C. G Wade

Two Decades and a Lustrum

Sunset of the Nineteenth Century

C. G Wade

Two Decades and a Lustrum
Sunset of the Nineteenth Century

ISBN/EAN: 9783744746885

Printed in Europe, USA, Canada, Australia, Japan

Cover: Foto ©Andreas Hilbeck / pixelio.de

More available books at **www.hansebooks.com**

TWO DECADES

AND

A LUSTRUM.

By C. G. WADE.

SUNSET OF THE NINETEENTH CENTURY.

By "JINGLING JOHNNIE."

(JUNIUS JUNIOR.)

LONDON:

MDCCCLXXVII.

It was said by the old monkish poet—

"Bella gerant alii, tu Felix Austria nubes."

It was well said, " Many and powerful have been the marriages contracted by the great Kaisers of the House of Hapsburg, but none have been so auspicious and happy as that of the present noble minded representative of the House of Hapsburg. A marriage of pure, simple love and affection. It brought no accrete or addition of wealth or power, but it brought the lofty, refined spirit and bright intelligence that has, in concert with her Kaiser, and the aid of faithful and devoted servants like the Count Von Beust and Andrassy, won the love and loyalty of the high spirited but freedom loving Hungarian people, and installed her as Empress indeed of all her people.

The march winds blew keen, when to visit our shore,
To share in our sport, a fair Empress came o'er;
How chilly and cheerless to her must have seemed
Our climate, but warm hearts its coldness redeemed.

Soon again may her presence our hearts make rejoice,
Soon again may we hear her sweet musical voice;
In our sports and our pastimes we'll take a new pride,
When again such a guest shall deign with us ride.

CONTENTS.

PREFACE.

ALL frequenters of our law courts, and those familiar with the cost of criminal procedure and the practice pursued, are well aware that the first step of the prosecuting counsel is to prove motive, and that if the prisoner pleads guilty, he may instruct counsel to be heard in mitigation of sentence, and to plead extenuating circumstances. "Qui s'excuse s'accuse," and I fear I must plead guilty, and throw myself on the mercy of the Court, when I stand at the bar of Public Opinion, arraigned on the very grave and serious charge of spoiling good paper with bad verses, I will not presume to call it poetry. "The Judges have met—a terrible show," and to save the time of the Court and the prosecuting counsel, Serjeants Critic and Cynic, Q.C., I will admit the motive, the commission of the felonious act, and plead in mitigation of my sentence the honesty of the purpose which led me to commit the offence.

The object for which I write these rude rhymes, and the ends and aims which I have kept steadily in view, and which alone nerved me to take the fatal plunge of rushing into print, and, probably, making myself a laughing-stock, was and is to try and strike the key-note—like a rude and rough pioneer, to prepare the way for the gradual instilling into the minds of the leaders and guides of Public Opinion the absolute paramount necessity of universal compulsory military service. If the press will only take up the question and not cease until it has by them been borne into the minds of the whole nation, that it is a question which cannot be shirked or put off, but that we must make up our minds one way or other. One year's drill, not desultory and spasmodic, but hard, unceasing schooling in the use of arms, constant exercise in the field, and the daily being called to assist in battalion and brigade manœuvres, is an education in itself. Habits of order and method, of politeness and punctuality, of absolute unquestioning obedience to orders, of the stern necessity for steadiness and sobriety, these are the lessons taught by even one year of the iron discipline of barrack life. It is the greatest possible mistake to suppose that a year's service prevents a youth from getting on in life; it is the finest rough and ready education in the world. It gives a graceful carriage; an upright, easy walk—a great contrast to the slouching and bent back, and stooping shoulders and contracted chest of those who have never been "set up." The moral and social benefits which accrue from universal military service are the mingling of classes otherwise far apart: they learn to know each other: the men begin to find their officers are not what the demagogues and radical carpet-baggers and spouters would fain represent them to be, but men like unto themselves, taking an interest in their men, sharing their hopes and cares, their joys and sorrows; ever ready to help them out of a difficulty, to make excuses for them when they have got into a scrape, to warn and caution them, and use all their influence to keep them straight. As for the officers themselves, universal military service has raised the standard very high in Germany. There, an officer only becomes one by his own merit and attainments; he has not only to attain to and come up to, but he has to retain and preserve intact the very high standard which is the measurement of a German officer. These men, having gone through the stern ordeal of drill and discipline in all its phases, from the goose-step to the drilling of a brigade, become an institution; the officer is recognised wherever he goes as a man who has realised the fact that he has duties and responsibilities quite beyond and outside his own private self and selfish interests; duties which his conscience will not permit him to shirk or evade. We English have never sufficiently realised the fact that each of us as a citizen and member of the great nation to which he belongs, is bound to qualify himself in every way, and render himself efficient and capable to protect and defend and do good service for his country, which has provided for him and enabled him to earn an honest living, if poor, or protected his property if rich. Prince Albert, that good, and wise, and deeply loved and lamented Prince, saw and suggested all this; but he was so modest and unassuming; so careful never to even seem to dictate. That mild and gentle Prince was very slow to tender his advice on any matter of state, and most wisely held aloof from politics. Once and once only he did travel out of his usual course, and warned us we did not know what we were about when we quarrelled with our old and natural ally, Russia, and bade us think twice, and thrice, before we joined an "imbroglio," the end and issue of which he could not see. How impatiently we listened, or rather refused to listen, is now a matter of history. The soundness of his advice was proved too late for us to profit by it. Let us take warning, and while yet it is not too late let us lay to heart and not let fall to the ground his advice as to universal military service. The passing through the ranks and service under the colours would be a sort of universal going to college and taking a degree. If a

youth served his time with credit and reputation, the
stamp of good conduct would be set on him for his
future career.   The physique of our rising generation
would undoubtedly be greatly improved.   Regular
hours, constant exercise, enforced habits of sobriety,
and good regular meals, must tell their tale, and
give vigour and strength at the most critical age,
when a growing lad most requires plenty of good
food, sleep, and exercise.   If I can succeed in
merely arousing a faint quaver, and just touch the
key-note, the wakeful, sensitive ear of the press may
vibrate responsive to it.   This key-note, struck ever
so lightly, is all we want; the press will soon take it
up.   That great guide and leader of Public Opinion
will gradually educate the people.   As Disraeli
educated his party to household suffrage, so will the
press gradually enure and reconcile us to the idea of
ultimately recognizing the absolute necessity and
expediency of universal military service.   Our press
is not venal, neither is it "inspired or officious."
No doubt various papers represent various sections
of parties and politics, and likewise the financial

interests of the proprietors have to be studied, they must be made to pay; nevertheless there is hardly a single English newspaper that will not go out of its way to expose rascality and corruption, and that will not be prepared to pay for so exposing it. A hundred instances can be shown of vast litigation, involving almost ruinous costs, incurred by newspapers who fearlessly exposed and held up to public gaze acts of malversation, corruption or vice. It is now for the press to direct the thoughts of the English people to the fact that they have hitherto shirked their duties as citizens, and by recognizing that fact, and personally fulfilling them, millions may be saved to the country. Taxation may be reduced more than one-half, the tone and "morale" of our whole population, high or low, socially and physically, greatly improved, and raised to a much higher standard. The "Battle of Dorking" was a kind of prophetic warning. The late discussions in both Houses have only shown the utter bewilderment of luckless ministers whenever they had to take up the question of "how to provide a proper supply of soldiers." Captain Hine's pamphlet "Universal Conscription: the only Answer to the Recruiting Question," completes the effect of the "Battle of Dorking," and, combined with the fruitless scheming of two successive ministers of war, Lord Cardwell and Mr. Gathorne Hardy, both equally zealous in the cause, have left in the minds of men a kind of preparation to entertain the idea of universal military service.

My object is to render popular, and to convey in a popular form, the seemingly dry, but, in reality, highly interesting succession of facts and factors of motives and movers of causes and effects, of failures and successes which, "tottled" up together make the sum of the history of the last twenty-five years. In all our surprising efforts and persistent attempts "not to do it," nothing is so astounding as our praiseworthy, but mistaken struggles in the direction of that department of social economy called education. Any boy or girl of ordinary capacity can, before the age of sixteen, by the exercise of their faculties and attention to their studies, easily become a fairly elegant scholar, familiar, if a boy, with the beauties of Sophocles, Homer, and Euripides; if a girl, with the classic poetry of Tasso, Dante, Béranger, Schiller, and Gœthe. The want or deficiency in their studies is at once apparent, and becomes lamentably and ridiculously conspicuous in their utter ignorance of more recent and contemporary modern history to receive and retain a lasting impression of historical events when conveyed in the more pleasing form of poetry: the Siege of Troy would never have become famous save for the muse of Homer. The founders of Rome would have been unknown save for Virgil. Her luxury and civilization in the plenitude of her power are revealed alone by Horace, Juvenal, and Martial. Macaulay's "Lays of Ancient Rome" have made many a boy and girl turn again with interest and an eager spirit of inquiry to Gibbon or Niebuhr, whose pages seemed so dull and wearisome before; the jingle of the verse has touched the keynote, and the mind is attuned for the diligent perusal of history. Sir Walter Scott's " Lay of the

Last Minstrel" has suddenly inspired his young worshipper with the desire to know the circumstances which made the Douglas an exile, and to learn which among Scotland's kings was "the Knight of Snowdoun;" the "Tales of my Grandfather," are taken down, and its pages no longer skimmed over desultorily, but pored over with absorbing interest. Thus is the poet a pioneer to his more grave and sedate brother the historian. Old Herodotus did quite right in making the muses a group of inseparables. The poet, the historian, the travelled geographist, the logarithm-weaving calculating problem-solving astronomer, the dramatist and play writer, and finally the actor, all are soldiers fighting in the same cause, of education, enlightenment, and elevation of the mind. Poets, musicians, actors, and, I fear, authors, are looked upon in this material, utilitarian age, as not "practical." To use the words of the hard men of business, "It does not pay." I believe this is utterly untrue, and is only the view of men, whose vision is limited to the one object ever before their eyes—money-making. They do not see that many of their fellows are able to take far clearer and keener views of things than themselves, simply because their minds have been raised and refined, and their thoughts elevated by more intellectual aspirations, albeit, " disgracious in the City's eyes." The spirit of Shakespeare, will sometimes visit the murkiest of mammon-worshipping counting-houses.

> " It is the precious province of true thought
> Of the divine creations of the mind,
> To live unwearied in a heart o'er wrought
> By busy intercourse with town mankind."

To return, therefore, to my original theme, that poetry, however rude, is the best vehicle in which history can take a lift when she is foot-sore and leg-weary. Let that grave and plodding pedestrian not despise the most jolting of tumbrils, the most creaking of carts; the waggoner, though a boor in a smock frock, may cheer his team by chaunting some old song, which, when enquired into, turns out to be a fragment of a country-side legend or tradition, which supplies a missing link in a nation's annals. Such for instance, was the old Cornish popular song of

"Tre and Pol and Pen." It recorded and rescued from oblivion a chapter in history. In Wales, it is in the writer's recollection, only four years ago, no inn or hotel of any repute was without its harper, who sat in the entrance hall and played the national instrument, the harp. The bards were not bards only in name, they were real children of song and poetry, full of ancient lore and traditions of the wild Welch of other days. The "March of the men of Harlech," "The curse of the Bard on King Edward the First," conveyed in that most beautiful of old melodies

> "Ruin seize thee, ruthless king,
> Confusion on thy banners wait."

heard for the first time in a Welch inn, haunted the memory of many a youth and maiden, until they were led to pull down the long neglected "Mrs. Markham," and a spirit of enquiry once awakened, the muse of history holds the reader in her thrall. This is the *raison d'etre*, and thus originated those "*Eisteddfods*," or musical festivals, which have become so popular and successful throughout the principality. Thus the "refrain" of an old Welch air has vibrated unresponded to for centuries, until at last it has woke up an echo that has been caught up and repeated, until a responsive chorus of congenial spirits have preserved and perpetuated it as one of the national melodies of Wales, which first led her children to appreciate their country's literature, and rescue from oblivion and neglect her history, her language, and her customs. So is it in nearly all countries : the national airs and national songs are all an accurate index to the national mind, they are all worthy of investigation and enquiry. Out of the tens of thousands of the thousands who have enriched their minds and gladdened their eyes with the lovely landscapes and delicious scenery of Loch Katrine and Vennachar, the Trossachs, and Loch Lomond, what single one would have ventured so far afield, save for the wand of the wizard of the north that beckoned him on. Scotland had by no means given a favorable impression to her earlier visitors, and few had penetrated into her little known regions, save commercial travellers, bagmen, and the pioneers of commerce. Even these hardy adventurers, driven by the trade winds, by no means gave Caledonia a good character, their southern stomachs missed the strong ale and juicy joints they had been accustomed to south of the border, and grumbling, crusty, cross old Dr. Samuel Johnson, shook the dust off his feet as he came Londonwards, and when he found himself safely ensconced in the "Cheshire Cheese," after a walk down Fleet Street, and through Temple Bar, he gave the rough side of his tongue and his heartiest malediction on Scotland; and the Scotch Lowlanders and Highlanders all alike came under his categorical curse—"Marry good air beggars all"! "A change came o'er the spirit of this dream," and Caledonia, stern and wild, suddenly found herself invaded by an army of Southrons, not as formerly, with spear and sword, and brown bill, but a fair company of courteous lords and ladies, scholars and grave professors, antiquaries and archæologists, all with money in their purse and the will to spend it freely. We may date the

prosperity of Scotland from the time when Sir
Walter Scott's poetry and romances first became
really appreciated, and for the first time it dawned
upon the mind of the general public and people of
Great Britain that a heaven-born genius had been
sojourning unknown and unrecognized in the far
north, and Scotland had been " entertaining an
angel unawares." The broad rich Doric, spoken
not only by the peasantry and lower classes, but by
the lairds and gentry, had been sneered at previously,
and Robert Burns' beautiful homely songs had
remained a sealed book to all, save those who could
appreciate the merits of " braid Scots." The
cipher only wanted the key, and the hitherto puzzled
and benighted Southron had in despair thrown on
one side, " We're nae that fou, but just a drappie
in our e'e," exclaiming, more in sorrow than in
anger, " these people sing and speak in vowels and
monosyllables ! " The thrilling narratives of " The
Antiquary," " The Heart of Mid Lothian," and
" Guy Mannering," soon brought " braid Scots," into
the list of civilized languages, and recognized as a

peculiarly graphic, descriptive, terse meaning-con-
veying, expressive dialect, chiefly derived from our
Swedish and Scandinavian ancestors. I may here
remark, that any sportsman or tourist who seeks
" fresh fields and pastures new," amid the fields and
fiords of Norway or Sweden, has only to take
up his abode at Buckie (short for Buckhaven), or
Peterhaven, or in the parts about Aberdeen, and do a
little sketching among the fishing folk and " caller
herring," and *rizzard* or smoked haddock dealers and
curers, to become a fair Scandinavian scholar, when
he lands at Christiana, or Bergen, he would be able
to talk to the " bonder " in their own vernacular.

From the " Poet's Corner," therefore, we may
safely conclude, first emanated the spirit of enquiry
and research, and the desire of information as to
the history, customs, and language of Scotland. We
have heard of Wales. Both countries and both
peoples have been won over from the instinctive
hostility of races, language and creed, to a perfect
union and inseparable amalgamation. We await
the coming man, the Heaven-born poet of the

future, who shall teach us English, Welch, and
Scotch, to learn to take an interest in the language,
history, and traditions of our Irish neighbours, we
shall then find in them the same interest, beauties of
imagery and ideal thought, as seen by Nature to
have been implanted in the breast of Nature's
children everywhere.

PROLOGUE.

" Let critic harsh and sage severe reprove

Our humble efforts to please ; do you remove

Our fears of faltering feet, and halting rhyme.

O gentle reader, smile, and take it all in time."

WAR IN HUNGARY.

B

WAR IN HUNGARY.

THE Emperor Francis Joseph, on the 1st May, 1849, headed in person the forlorn hope at the storming of Raab, in Hungary. Five-and-twenty years after-wards, on the anniversary of that day, he was invested by the Emperor of Russia with the order of the Knights of St. George, Russian Legion of Honour decoration. This celebration of that anni-versary was rendered more remarkable by the fact that those five-and-twenty years had been spent by the Kaiser Francis Joseph in patiently winning over to him his various subjects, who had only been estranged from him by the insiduous wiles and schemes of cosmopolitan adventurers and dema-gogues, whose business as professional agitators, was to throw down the apple of discord between a generous prince and a loyal people. Nothing ought to be more painful to Englishmen who think and see for themselves, and are not carried away by igno-rant prejudices and crude opinions formed in the absence of reliable data, than our conduct at the time of the War in Hungary. Austria had been an

old and faithful ally. The Austrian army was
largely officered by Englishmen. Hungary was a
terra incognita to most of us. We however accepted,
as we are so unfortunately wont to do, the mere
ipse dixit of an unknown adventurer, Kossuth,
merely because he made bold and sweeping assertions, entirely unsupported by evidence. A brave
old soldier, Haynau, came over to visit England,
and, while out of curiosity visiting one of our great
brewing establishments, he was set upon by a troop
of giant draymen and mobbed. Nothing could be
more disgraceful, nothing more cowardly. Our big,
burly brewers' men are too manly to have done such
a thing of their own heads, and of course were put
up to it by some contemptible radical clerk, who
was ass enough to believe that all must be gospel
that was in print. Any one who knew anything of
the subject was quite aware that all the absurd
canards about "Tiger" Haynau were impudent
inventions, without the slightest shadow of founda-
tion. The lamentable civil war in Hungary, which
turned a smiling garden flowing with milk and
honey into a wilderness, was a great event in history. It was kindled, no doubt, into actual fire, by
the sparks emanating from the great revolutionary
explosion in France, which fired the train already
laid by ambitious demagogues to every capital and
city in Europe. As far as I could make out on the
spot, Hungary had no real grievance to complain of,

no oppressive acts at the hands of their Government; her people were exceptionally prosperous, but Protestant, and followers of Huss, who suffered martyrdom in 1415; they had their own parish priest, and their whole system of internal economy resembled our own England nearer than any other country. The Concordat at that time had not been granted, the magnates and noblemen of Hungary were smitten with quite an Anglo-mania, and everything English was the fashion of the day. How a needy adventurer like Kossuth could possibly spoil all this, and throw down all the long-accumulated pile of prosperity, is one of those questions that can only be solved by the answer, "that nothing goes down with the general mass so well as to be told they have a grievance." I had the honour and pleasure of the personal acquaintance of some of the leading spirits of the Insurrection; they, however, were no adventurers, they had large possessions and held a great stake in the country: like Stonewall Jackson and General Robert Lee in the great civil war in America, between the North and South, it cost them a sore struggle and a wrestling and agony of the spirit before they could make up their minds with which party it was their duty to throw in their lot. That decision once taken they faltered not, they cast the hazard on the die and stood to it. The Emperor of Austria and his Government have, in a rare and large-hearted spirit of conciliation and forgiveness, recognized all this; Deak,* Andrassy, and all the great leaders of the Insurrection of '48, are now ministers. Kossuth, simply, was a very clever, plausible adventurer, with a marvellous gift of the gab. He had gauged off the enthusiastic patriotism of all the people from the highest to the lowest. An enthusiasm that, if it had been evoked in a better cause, would be entitled to the warmest admiration. The brave, enthusiastic character of the people of Hungary and Poland, very like our Irish in their temperament, renders them peculiarly impressionable and open to the machinations of designing demagogues, who know how to effect their purpose by instilling vague, wild notions of wrong and oppression, and turn the glowing patriotism of the brave people to their own selfish purposes, and to advance their own private interests. Like the Irish people and Dan O'Connell, "Kossuth said so, and what Kossuth said must be true." Hardly any of the insurgents knew what they were fighting for; the Hönveds and Hussars who did the actual fighting, when reproached for being in arms against their Emperor, all gave the same reply, evidently an honest one,—"We are fighting for our Kaiser, but the German Generals want to give our lands to the Croats!" Some of the Chiefs who commanded in the army of the Insurgents were men of great capacity. As is always the case in civil war,

* Since dead.

the military leaders, who ought to be absolute
dictators, were interfered with by Kossuth, the
civilian; and instead of the campaign being con-
ducted by one head, and all the rest being parts of
one harmonious whole, the plans of Görgey, Bem,
and Dembinski, were frustrated and defeated by
Kossuth's interference. There is a very beautiful
picture, the subject of which is, " Last Thoughts of
Hungary." The study of the noble features of these
great and gifted leaders, Bem and Dembinski, those
two " death-defying Poles," Klapka (in after time,
in common with General Williams, one of the
defenders of Kars), Guyon, an Englishman, and
Görgey, a man of astonishing strategical powers,
makes one sigh over the sad fate that impelled these
men to turn their swords against their Emperor and
their Government, and die exiles in a foreign
land, instead of living to lead on their gallant
soldiers against a foreign foe and invader. Had
such men as Bem and Dembinski commanded,
Solferino might have been a Novara. We may
indeed say with Sir Walter Scott, who sighed to
think that Flodden might have been a Bannockburn
if the Scottish forces had been led as they were on
that glorious day:

" O Görgey, for thy leader's staff,
Fierce Guyon for thy speed ;
O for one hour of Klapka's wight,
Or well-skilled Bem to rule the fight,

And cry, " Our Kaiser and our right! "
Another sight had seen that morn,
From Fate's dark book a leaf been torn,
And Austria crowned with victory ! "

———————————

Danube, Danube, once so blue,
Wherefore hast thou changed thy hue ?
When in thee my hands I'd lave,
Shrink I back from gory wave ?

Oh ! rejoice, thou dark Euxine,
Darker are my waves than thine ;
Black Sea wast thou called before,
Blacker shalt thou be with gore.

Once my river's stagnant flow
Glided past with current slow,
Sleepy hamlets, prosperous town,
Drowsy cots my banks did crown,
Village bells my murmurs drown.

Now the tocsin sounds from far,
" Havoc! " cries the Dog of War ;
Flaming village, smoking town,
Now my banks all gleaming crown.

Sclave and death-defying Pole
Corpses down my current roll :
Fierce Magyar and swarthy Hun
Darker still my current dun.

Böhmisch giants, curassiers ;
Lancers with tough ashen spears ;
All in one red carnage blent,
Corpses now, their life is spent.

By Danube, when the sun was low,
White the sands as driven snow,
When the drums beat at dead of night,
Then Danube saw another sight.*

Priests and Demagogues united
    Have done their work, and wide
Is the breach 'tween Prince and People,
    That from each their hearts divide.

And the chivalrous young monarch,
    So kind, and ever fain
To hear his meanest subject's prayer,
    Who never prayed in vain ;

* See " Battle of Hohenlinden."

He would not to the vulgar crowd
Yield what they craved with clamour loud.
Foul wrong he's had from sland'rous tongue,
Foul wrong from priest, from rebels wrong.

'Twas for thee, sage Saxon statesman,
    'Twas for thee the glorious *role*,
To weld these warring elements
    Into one homogenous whole ;

'Tween the Kaiser and his Paladins,
    So loyal and so brave,
All the differences of race and creed
    To bury in one grave.

All memories of quarrels past
    Are quenched in love so true,—
" *Pro lege nostro moriamur*,"—
    We'll live and die for you.*

My fierce heart beat so wildly !
    E'en now it angers me
That to crafty plotting schemers
    Thou hast bent thy gallant knee !

*The cry of the Magyar nobles when they rallied round
Maria Thérèsa.

Thy blooming youth all blighted,
And thy nature fresh and free,
With Concordat, Comminations.
And tricks of grammarye.

Now the mists are fast dissolving
That obscured thine honest eyes,
And with clear and undimmed vision
Thou gazest on the skies.

No more clouds shall come between us;
Lean on thy people's breast;
Trust in Providence serenely,
And calmly take thy rest.
Thy loving people bless thee,
And thou shalt e'en be blest!

When the Kaiser Francis Joseph was crowned King of
Hungary in 1867, when Andrassy and Francis Deak (aided by
Pulsky) brought about the great reconciliation between the
Kaiser of Austria and his long-estranged people, he refused
to accept the usual tribute paid on the accession of a new
king to the throne of Hungary; and when it was forced on
him as the customary tribute of Hungarian people to the king
of Hungary, he only accepted it on condition that it should be
handed over to the wounded and invalided " Hönveds " who
had suffered in the war when they took up arms against their
Kaiser. A " Chelsea Hospital," or " Hôtel des Invalides,"
was founded with this money. Could forgiveness and conciliation go further?

CHARLES ALBERT ON THE MORROW OF NOVARA.

CHARLES ALBERT ON THE MORROW

OF NOVARA.

ITALY lay bound and helpless after Novara,

> " In mute despair,
> Tearing with gyve-worn hand her blood-bedraggled hair,"

clutching a dagger in her feeble, fevered grasp, henceforward to brood helplessly over her wrongs un-
avenged, and her efforts baffled and paralysed ; no
practical or probable hope of revenge save in the
stiletto of the assassin.   Suddenly from her dark
broodings she is roused by the sound of heavy foot-
steps—a long determined stride : they echo through
the corridors of the lonely prison-house ; nearer and
yet more near they come ; the door is opened, and
the Deliverer appears !   His mask is down, and in
the darkness the brain-sick captive can only see a
shadowy, indistinct form ; but that form leans over
her, and whispers comfort.   The captive thinks that
in her dire extremity there has indeed at last descended some heaven-sent spirit of grace and mercy.
But suddenly a bright and almost blinding radiant

beam of sunshine pierces through the barred and stanchion-bound casement, and its golden effulgence reveals the face of her deliverer. No delicate, white-winged messenger this from other far-off worlds ; but a very real, substantial, human form of flesh and blood. The ruddy genial cheeks and bright eyes of Cavour beam all benignantly on the pale and trembling captive ; he bids her arise and stand up : like the angel to St. Peter he saith, " Arise up quickly." She did arise, and she now walks alone and unsupported ; but her deliverer has gone up aloft, to join the shining throng of patriot spirits. " *Italia fara da se.*"

Mourn, mourn, ye Patriots, mourn,
For comrades overborne !
For gyves and chains still worn ;
Poor fettered freedom, mourn !

Radetsky's serried ranks,
Sclavonians, Teutons, Franks ;
Oh ! who has e'er withstood
Such vast o'erwhelming flood
Of Vandal, Goth, and Hun ?

It boots not now to say
" We should have altered our array,

And changed our front!"   Too late,
We saw our ranks give way
On that dread and fatal day,
When to veteran war-worn foes
We'd the folly to oppose
Those levies, raw and green.

When the tug of war was seen,
And Greek met Greek, I ween
Full soon their martial ire,
Like hay or straw on fire,
Was quenched in flight's desire,
Wild and disorderly :
Little qualified to meet
Those foeman, stern and wild !

" Break, break, my bursting heart !
These o'erstrained cords now part.
Too solid flesh, dissolve !
Thaw and resolve thyself.

For how can monarch ride
His gallant chiefs beside?
My lofty hopes are hushed,
My battered helm is crushed,

My broken sword is rust,
My honour's in the dust.

My soul will to the saints, I trust,
Nor more for life I lust,
Leave now this world I must ;
My country to my God I trust,
Italia, now, good night ! "

· The dying Monarch smiled ;
Whispered an angel mild,
So sweetly and so low.
Hark ! to the unearthly strain,
Like softly dropping rain
It trills upon his ear.

He sees you white-robed messenger,
Beckoning with accents mild,
" Well done, thou faithful child !
Soldier, rest thee ! rest, O rest thee !
Here no bugle sounds réveillée ;
Sleep the sleep that knows no waking,
Here's no drum thy slumbers breaking.

Not in vain thy sacrifice,
Whom affliction did baptize ;

Pleased the Almighty to chastise,
Sanctified and purified
In dark sorrow's burning tide.

Rise, thou good and faithful King,
In thy need I comfort bring."

See a gallant Son arise,
Well I mark his father's eyes ;
Thou shalt be this hero's shield,
He'll his father's falchion wield
O'er full many a well-fought field.

Thou, unseen, invisible,
Spirit pure and essence thin,
Thou shalt soar o'er battle din,
His guardian angel thou.

Thou shalt turn the bursting shell,
Thou shalt guard his sword-arm well,
As of old the heroes twain,
Castor and Pollux, twins germane,
On Lake Regillus' shore
The barbarous hosts o'erbore,
And sudden panic struck ;

So, too, shalt thou, in spirit be,
Leading the flower of chivalry
At Solferino's field.

Behind, a brighter hour impends ;
Italia's star full blaze ascends :
Free-thought old Superstition rends,
The Bourbon quakes, poor Bomba bends,
A suppliant for his throne.
Fulfilled at last, Cavour, thy boast,
Italia's free from coast to coast ;
From Alpine height to Apennine,
All, all is free—all, all is thine.
Fara da se, Italia !

COUNT CAVOUR IN 1850.

COUNT CAVOUR IN 1850.

WE are told in a beautiful hymn that

> " God works in a mysterious way,
> His wonders to perform ; "

and from time to time Providence raises up great instruments to do His work. These great men only make their appearance at dates few and far between, when the life and welfare of a particular people or nation would seem to depend on some such providential interposition. Such Heaven-sent patriot was our own Cromwell; such was Washington for America; such was Cavour for Italy. Dark and dismal, indeed, were the days of Italy when Cavour's brain began to work. He had hitherto been only a genial, ruddy-faced, pleasant man of the world, using his keen wits in now and then making a hit on the Bourse: always a welcome guest everywhere. Suddenly the celestial fire descended and touched him ; he awoke to see his country as she was, stricken down after the fatal day of Novara, with her noble warrior-king, Charles Albert, dead. If ever man died of a broken heart, then Charles Albert (a giant in stature, strength, and courage) did, an exile at Lisbon. Austria, slowly recovering from the terrible wounds she had received in the great internecine struggle with Hungary, had tightened her hold on Italy's neck, and had held every town and district with troops that could not but recall with bitterness how they had been jeered and insulted in the days of Austria's reverses by the half " Moblet " volunteers and mobs with muskets in their hands. Kossuth and the demagogues had done their work, and had estranged a loyal, contented people from a true, chivalrous and liberal-hearted monarch. No light anywhere for Italy : no sympathy. The Milan free corps and swaggering *café* loungers, who turned tail at Novara, and rendered vain the valour of Charles Albert and his gallant Piedmontese, had disgusted the world with Italy. Liberator Cavour was just beginning to gain the confidence of his king, the gallant son of a gallant father, Victor Emanuel, "*Il Re Galantuomo,*" when the war between Russia and Turkey began. As soon as France and England intervened, and took the part of the " Sick Man," his clear, prescient, far-seeing mind, at once detected that it was a logical sequence, that if a Christian power intervened to come to the assistance of an infidel and alien race, then a Christian power might intervene and come to the assistance of a fellow-Christian and cognate race; and that France and England, who had listened and paid attention to the cries for help of a Moslem, and half-Asiatic, and autocratic dynasty, could not turn a deaf ear to the tears and entreaties of a free, constitutional, enlightened people, nearly akin in race, blood, and language. Cavour strengthened his position by requesting permission to send an Italian contingent to the allied armies banded together to resist the aggressive designs of Russia. His request was granted, and a most carefully selected and very perfectly equipped contingent left Spezzia for the shores of the Crimea. These men were the flower of the army of the united kingdom of Piedmont and Sardinia, then a small and miniature state. Cavour knew that this entitled him to have a seat and a voice at the board of the council of Europe whenever the war came to an end, and when the time arrived for making final arrangements for keeping the peace on the Continent. All he expected came to pass exactly as he had foreseen. The gallantry and devotion of the Sards and Piedmontese at Traktir earned for them a high reputation and military prestige. Every one of his prognostications was verified, and from that hour the northern little mountain state of Piedmont, known as the kingdom of the Two Sardinias, became a factor among the great figures that make up the sum of Europe; no longer a cipher, but an admitted and acknowledged active element and institution.

Our own statesman, Mr. Gladstone, helped on
the great work, for he visited and exposed in
burning words, and in stirring and indignant
eloquence, all his own, the horrors of Neapolitan
prisons, the shocking cruelties perpetrated, and the
miseries undergone by the state political prisoners
in the dungeons of Naples.

All this paved the way for a gradual approach and
appeal to Napoleon II. and his *Idées Napoléonnines*
of nationalities, which that monarch, finding that
all was ripe, and that Italy was under the guidance
of a great statesman, who could safely be trusted at
the helm, accepted and undertook. Then came the
celebrated New-year's reception of the diplomatic
body, and Napoleon's stern accosting of the Austrian
Ambassador, who made his bow and retired. After
this followed Magenta, Montabella, and Solferino.
The temporary peace patched up at Villa Franca
over a cutlet and a cigar, was merely arranged from
Napoleon's horror at the bloody sights he had seen
at Solferino, and the natural desire of both monarchs
to stop the further terrible slaughter.

Cavour held his tongue and showed an admirable
patience, although probably full of bitter disappointment at seeing the work unfinished. He bided his
time, as he always had done. Soon, however, the
hour came, and the man Garibaldi and his red-
shirts sent Bomba to the right-about. Meanwhile
Cavour went on quietly preparing his country for

the great effort which he saw must be made while
Napoleon still ruled France.   Cavour saw that
France had only whetted her appetite for military
glory; that she had insufficient laurels in her
contest with Russia, when in good sooth the
Muscovite had stoutly held his own.   He saw that
she would throw down the gauntlet to Prussia, and
then the hour would come for Italy to strike again
for Venice and Rome.

'Twas in his lonely chamber that Cavour, deep in
    thought,
Sadly pondered o'er the future—little light the
    prospect brought,
And the shadows dark and gloomy that the gloaming
    cast athwart
The dim and latticed window, chilled the noble
    patriot's heart.

" If I westward cast my eyes, what meets my vision
    there ?
A dotard frail and feeble sits in the papal chair,

And Rome throned on her seven hills, where Em-
    perors erst did rule,
Sees a shaveling, false and feeble, ensconced upon
    his stool,
Mumble forth his pater noster, his '*Non possumus*—
    We can't;'
Soon in a voice of thunder we'll answer, 'No, you
    shan't!'

If my gaze I then turn eastward, what meets my
    vision there?
See Lombardy's fair plains, a prospect rich and
    rare,
See Milan's stately towers and her vast cathedral
    dome,
Only barracks for Tedeschi, and for barbarous
    Croats a home."

Thus meditating sadly, his eye fell on the wine,
Richly mantling in his goblet, fresh from its home
    grown vine.
" I pledge thee, O my country, thou sunny land of
    mine ! "
He raised the goblet to his lips to quaff the generous
    wine.

He raised the goblet to his lips, when hark! the
 loud tattoo,
And the drummers came all drumming, and fifes, a
 noisy crew;
Each lady with averted gaze, and down-drawn veil
 will meet
Men and officers white-coated as they swagger down
 the street.

He paled! 'twas but a moment, for soon his patriot
 pride
Rushed crimson to his forehead in a darkly flushing
 tide—
Rushed crimson to his temples; all chances he
 defied.
"My country! O my country; thou art a name
 alone,
What art thou, O my country! what art thou now
 but stone?"

He cast the cup, untasted, and broken at his feet;
"Thy juices for the foreigner, for me it is not meet
To drink and to be merry, while those sounds are in
 the street.

Oh! Marino Faliero, and ye Doges, who of old,
Rowed forth in stately galleys and dropped your
rings of gold!
Ye mighty dead arise, in spirit be with me,
And, with God and king assisting, Italia shall be
free.

Oh! Venetia, fair and beautiful, the ocean's wedded
bride,
How fallen are thy fortunes, how broken is thy pride!
No longer merchant navies deeply laden on thy tide
Cast their treasures on thy jetties, and at their
anchors ride."
He ceased, and rose triumphant, triumphant o'er his
gloom,
And looked like some grim warrior just risen from
the tomb.

KING WILLIAM OF PRUSSIA AND BENEDETTI.

KING WILLIAM OF PRUSSIA AND
BENEDETTI.

In the very crisis and pinch of the Franco-German war, when our relations with Germany were *très accentuées*, a one-sided meeting was called by certain foolish, impulsive individuals, who demanded, and made a great disturbance at not obtaining, the use of the Mansion House—a meeting to express sympathy with France, and their, forsooth, disapproval of the conduct of Germany! The then Lord Mayor and Corporation, with their usual common sense, and their still stronger sense of justice, refused the use of premises belonging to the public for the purposes of a few individuals who wanted to bring themselves into notoriety at the expense of the nation. The writer had organized a meeting, to be presided over by the highest in the land, to assure the Germans of the absolute neutrality of England, and of their admiration of the character of the Germans. It is fondly hoped any soreness may be removed that may have possibly been occasioned by the wild and random speeches of ignorant and unreasoning men, who have not taken the trouble of mastering facts and learning the truth for themselves. The Germans have not answered calumny with calumny, or misrepresentation with misrepresentation; they have patiently and gently submitted to be defamed; to time and to Providence they have trusted to vindicate the slanders on their names; but their English cousins must not be silent any longer, but must boldly stand forth and hail the dawn of peace, and greet united Germany.

" Germania needs no bulwarks, no towers along the steep:
 Her fortress is her children's love, so pure, so grand, so
  deep! "

'Twas to Ems' life-giving waters, where Dame
 Nature, kindly nurse!
Laughs at learned chemists' potions, and doctors'
 fee-filled purse,
And from her own prescription mixes med'cines
 strong and rare,
Crying, " Come ye all and drink me; drink deep and
 do not spare."

'Twas thither that the brave old King, to rest each
 war-worn limb,

Betook him, little thinking of war and warfare grim ;
Full of peace and peaceful visions of his children,
brave and fair,
Of his honoured, love-crowned home, and the sweet
affections there.

And he walked forth in the morning, and it made
his heart rejoice
To see the gay crowd cluster, and to hear their light-
some voice.

Lo! a courtier smart approaches, a Plenipo' so
bland,
From Paris is his mission, and he comes to make
demand :
" France shall dictate to the nations, and who dare
say her nay ? "
" Well, Germany is peaceful, if at peace remain she
may ! "

He turned him on his heel, and his proud head
bowed he low,
As he gave his scornful *congé* to the lacquey of his
foe.

And the loiterers who lingered to gaze upon the
scene

Thought how loyally he bore himself with majesty
serene.

And Germania heard with wonder, not unmixed
with secret awe,
How well her ruler ruled himself, and still obeyed
the law.

Well I ween had Royal William been but a peasant
clown,
The insult he'd have hurled back, and struck the
braggart down.

Germania heard the insult; she bared her strong
right arm,
She bid the beacon blaze abroad and sound the
war's alarm.

Right well her children answered—hark to the
gathering cry !
" Wave Rhineland ! all thy banners wave ! " West-
phalia makes reply.

" Up, Hesse and Nassau ! up ! arise ! the clarion's
note is high ;
Bayern and Pommern wake ! arise ! " Black Bruns-
wick makes reply.

BISMARCK: HIS CHARACTER.

BISMARCK: HIS CHARACTER.

In 1863, who so popular a theme of unpopularity, so heartily and universally abused, as Bismarck? Alone, unknown, unrecognised, save as a Country Squire, and as holding a subordinate administrative appointment, he had the courage to bell the cat and take the bull by the horns. Having all his plans cut and dried, and being prepared to stand the racquet and brave all, he knew that he must be the scapegoat, the "Sunden Bock," and be willing to be considered for a long time the mere mouthpiece and tool of the Royal and military party, the mere puppet put forward by the ultra-Conservative and old "Kreutz Zeitung" party. No one misconstrues or misinterprets him now! His ends, his aims, his objects, are all understood and appreciated now. His countrymen know that they are all one with him, that he certainly entertains no *arrière pensées,* that he has no private ambitions, no private and

personal aspirations, no self-seeking, nor vulgar,
mean, low hankerings, common to many great and
mighty men of statecraft: but that he is indeed the
spirit of great Germany, that great Fatherland so long
undefined, the genius of "Deutschland," embodied,
incarnate, and personified. Strong, bluff, bold: free-
hearted and healthy in *physique*, and genial and jocund
of temper; a slow, deep thinker; a calm reasoner.
The nearest approximation to him in history is
Cromwell, but a Cromwell all "guiltless of his
country's blood," purer and more unselfish in his
aims, but of the same strong, hard type, a type best
described as of "blood and iron." Washington is,
perhaps, a nearer approximation, but Washington
was of a milder, gentler stamp, whose *rôle* was
played on the boards of a very small stage, so to
speak; America, or rather Virginia, Pennsylvania,
and New England, were mere young colonies, to
whom the foolish old country had proved a harsh
step-mother, and which had been alternately neglected and bullied by the wrong-headed, short-
sighted clique, who held with so shaky a hand the
reins of government. Washington merely had to
take the command of hardy emigrants and back-
woodsmen, whose rifle was never out of their hands,
pioneers of the wilderness, inured to hardships and
endurance. With such men and such metal at
his back, and with such tools to work with, was it
anything very wonderful that he was able to success-

fully cope with, and ultimately overcome, mere
levies of foreign mercenary bands, mere paid " con-
dottieri," with no interest or soul in the struggle, or
care for ought save their pay ? Nevertheless, the
purity of their characters and disinterested devotion
to their country make these two patriots resemble
each other, and render them in their nature akin.
Like Cincinnatus, who after freeing Rome went
back to walk between the stilts of his plough, where
they first found him, so Washington retired again
to private life and the pursuit of agriculture when
his work was done and the Constitution proclaimed.
So Bismarck is never so happy as when marking
trees in the woods at Varsin. In our own time, and
in the epoch of nearly contemporary history, his
nearest type is Sir Robert Peel, that great statesman having for some thirty years been the idol and
mouthpiece and doughty champion of the old Tory
and ultra-Conservative party, not as a paid gladiator
or delegate, but from a pure and deeply-seated con-
viction that in serving that party he was best serving
the interests of his country. He advocated their
cause and fought their battles with the most devoted
self-sacrifice and courage, and with the most unflinching zeal. When his calm, far-seeing gaze and
penetrating vision had detected with a prophetic dis-
cernment that the time had at length arrived, and the
crisis come, for his party to make a great concession,
he at once made up his mind, and boldly threw over

and cast to the winds all doubts, and fears, and
hesitations.   He saw that Free Trade was no
political question, or a *casus belli* on which Conser-
vatives and Liberals should take their stand and
join issue, but that it was a mere commercial
experiment that the exigencies of the times required
should be tried ; a riddle that could only be read,
an enigma that could only be solved by events, and
results and circumstances attending the experiment.
Our vast and teeming population cried aloud with
an imperious voice for that experiment to be tried.
The Corn Laws had done their work, and had done
good and yeomanly service.   Protection had raised
up a hardy, contented rural population, a " bold
peasantry, their country's pride ! " had raised a
race of loyal, comfortable, thriving Bonifaces,
farmers, and yeomen, the very backbone of a kingdom, the thews and sinews of a nation.   Heaths
and moors, commons and waste lands, had been
enclosed; swamps and fens and marshes had been
drained ; foreshores and sandy dunes reclaimed ;
peats and mosses warped and pared and burned,
and a system of scientific agriculture and high
farming introduced, all under the fostering influence
of Protection, and the prospect of large gains which
will alone ever have charms to attract capital and
create surprise.   So far, so good !   Protection like
the monks of old, had done its work and done it
well, but like them, their work being done, their day

had come ; with both it was a case of " Fuit Ilion : " both had to make a bow and retire from the stage. As the population increased and mouths multiplied, so it stood to reason and became a logical sequence and capable of mathematical demonstration, that if 40 acres could supply sufficient bread for 400 mouths, as those mouths multiplied to 4000 so 40 acres would be insufficient, and it was not likely that the hungry millions would hear tell of vast plains in Russia and Poland, in Wallachia and Moldavia, of rolling prairies in Illinois and Wisconsin, and all the Far West, where the soil, two feet thick of rich black loam, would laugh with corn when tickled with the plough, where wheat was produced in such vast abundance that granaries and warehouses could not be built fast enough to store it,—was it likely they would shut their ears to such stories of abundance ? They did listen, they opened wide their ears, quickened to a keen sense of hearing by the pangs of hunger and an unfilled stomach ; they opened wide their famine-hollowed eyes at the recountal of these strange tales of fabulous and over-flowing abundance and unheard-of plenty. They listened and they learned, and they cried aloud with a voice so loud and shrill that, like the " Ancient Mariner " to the " Wedding Guest," he could not choose but hear. Sir R. Peel did hear ; he saw the time had indeed arrived, he saw that the great party he had so long served and led, did not appreciate the

situation ; he chose his part, he accepted his mission,
he did not flinch or shrink from the pains and
agonies of the wrenching asunder of the ties by
which his very heart-strings had been so long
lovingly intertwined with his party : that party did
not, alas ! sufficiently recognise the glorious self-
abnegation and self-sacrifice of the man. More
happy Bismarck! He too saw the time had come
for his party—the old " Kreutz Zeitung," ultra-
Conservative, Junker party—to make a great concession, to surrender all their most cherished and
valued rights and privileges and powers. The
master he served, the grand old King, knew the
honesty and loyalty and pride of his faithful servant,
and backed him with all his personal weight and
influence. All honour to the German, and especially
to the Prussian nobility and upper classes, who
recognised the situation and trusted implicitly to
the wisdom and prudence of their faithful champion,
and did not cover him with abuse as a traitor to his
party, or tax him with selling his friends, but
graciously and without reserve made the concessions
he advised, and yielded them not grudgingly, but
freely and cheerfully.

Our people have been too long accustomed to
the license and liberty of an utterly uncontrolled
self-will, to recognise, at the moment, the gross
neglect of a citizen towards his fellows and the State
of which he is a member, in not voluntarily coming

forward to learn the use of arms, so that he may be qualified to lend his aid in defending his country in her hour of need. Universal education will teach this, and universal compulsory military service is only the logical sequence and complement of universal compulsory education. The one shows the citizen whom it has taught that he is not doing his duty to the State which has given him that priceless benefit of education, unless he shows his gratitude by qualifying himself to defend the giver ; that the chivalrous and noble nature of man, which has long been undeveloped and lain hidden as it were under a bushel, when lit up by education and intelligence. purified by a free religion, and disciplined by habits of order and method, attains a far higher standard of excellence than has yet been reached. Germany has learnt by the hard lessons of adversity, taught by the First Napoleon, that man must stoop to conquer, and that the meanest individual in a State has not only his own selfish interests to attend to, but has to give them up cheerfully and willingly for the good of the State and body politic of which he is a member. The ancient legend so well known throughout Germany, of the Emperor Barbarossa sunk down in an enchanted sleep, surrounded by warriors, has an exact resemblance to the tradition current on the Tweed, and made the subject of a most beautiful poem by Sir Walter Scott—" The Shepherd's Tale."

I marked a stalwart figure that long had pondering
    stood,
Sober and stern he seemed of cheer, immutable of
    mood,
And he gazed upon a picture, a picture strange and
    rare,—
The Kaiser Barbarossa and his mailèd hosts were
    there.

As he gazed upon the picture, he deep within him
    thought,
" What means this ancient legend ? " and all around
    him sought
For some way to read the riddle, but his brain no
    answer brought,
Till at length he rose inspired, dilated his huge size,
The sense of power grandly beaming in quiet from
    his eyes :

" Ho ! 'tis clear to me as noonday,—how could I e'er
    have sought
So widely for its meaning, when so close at hand 'tis
    brought ?
The parable is plain, the metaphor not deep,
Ignorance and Superstition cast down in death-like
    sleep

The might of mighty nations, and o'er their senses
creep
A dull and torpid lethargy, and their souls in slumber
steep.

Education is the watchword that shall rouse the
sleeping host,
Drill and discipline the ordeal that shall quell the
foeman's boast.
The chivalry of old shall wed with free, untrammeled
thought,
Intelligence and discipline shall to the work be
brought.
Patience and abnegation of self, and devotion to
others,
These, Holy Fatherland, shall make thee a nation
of brothers.

From the dawning of creation and its ages past, I
ween,
No people so united and so strong has e'er been seen.
Dost think that when unto the plough this hand is
put, I'll turn
To the follies of this foolish world ?   All pleasures
light I spurn.

With these mighty ends before me, these objects
    great in view,
I'll scorn all else beside, to one steady purpose true.

Deutschland, Deutschland, Uberalles! my waking
    thoughts at night ;
Deutschland, Deutschland, Uberalles ! my thoughts
    at morning bright."
As the meaning dawned upon him of the legend old
    and wild,
His heart swelled high within him, and he wept like
    any child.

" 'Tis mine to speak the watchword, 'tis for me to
    dare and do :
'Tis for me the mighty task to bring the legend true !
Soon the day shall dawn for Europe, and our Kaiser
    King shall ride
With Deutschland's flag united, his gallant chiefs
    beside.

Yes, our gallant Kaiser Wilhelm shall from the
    mountain's side
Issue forth with steel-clad squadrons, and through
    the nations ride.

He shall ride forth with his freeborn knights through
  all the fettered lands ;
And at his voice so loud and free shall burst the
  Papal bands.

The mill grinds very slowly, but it grinds exceeding
  small,
Prince and peasant, high and lowly, skilled warriors
  one and all.
When schoolmaster and drill-serjeant have done
  their work in full,
And the bands of iron discipline hold all in iron
  rule ;
When level for the charge Germania's arms are laid,
Where lives the desperate foe that e'er such onset ·
  stayed ? "

LOUIS NAPOLEON'S DEPARTURE FOR SEDAN.

LOUIS NAPOLEON'S DEPARTURE FOR SEDAN.

In Louis Napoleon England had a true friend, both in peace and war, and no relations ever existed between two nations, as far as he was concerned, so loyal and true. After the Crimean War, where the French had seen our weakness, just as the Prussians did that of the Austrians during the Danish campaign, our demagogues took the opportunity of doing everything they could to insult and outrage the Emperor, and through him the French nation and army. One of our most vulgar and blatant, noisy, brazen Buzfuzes, made an absurd, catch-penny, pot-house speech in defence of Dr. Bernhard and the Orsini, who had openly counselled and publicly advised through their organs the assassination of Louis Napoleon. This contemptible snob had a sort of penny, tawdry ovation among the refugees and scum of Leicester Square. His clap-trap, balderdash speech, was translated and fully reported in all the continental journals. The French were justly, and with ample reason,

hurt and offended, and nothing but the admirable
tact and discretion of Lord Palmerston, and the
firm loyalty to us of Louis Napoleon, prevented our
being attacked; and thus this great country, its
peace, its prosperity, and all its future, were put in
jeopardy and deadly peril by the wretched balderdash and windy rubbish of an ass like this, who put
himself forward, forsooth, as the mouthpiece of
England and Magna Charta! England apparently
likes being humbugged, or, rather, John Bull is so
honest that he believes all his children are so.

TWENTY years of piping, prosperous peace! full
    twenty years had flown,
And Napoleon the silent sat watching on his throne.
When Anarchy awoke, all reeking from her lair.
She blinked and curst God's sunshine; she curst
    God's balmy air;

She scowled at steady stripling; she scowled at
    modest maid;
She joined each ribald witling to sneer at matron
    staid.
She scowled at laughing children, they shuddered
    and grew cold;

She scowled at merry maidens; she scowled at
    young and old ;
She scowled at honest workmen, home trudging
    from their toil,
And to see their honest faces it made her black
    blood boil.

She scowled till she grew frantic, for in her heart
    was gloom ;
She looked not 'cross the Atlantic, where for all
    there's ample room.
" We've had enough of labour, and enough of toil
    have we,
Henceforth to knife and sabre give all till we be free.

Our rulers and employers against us are arrayed ;
Statesmen, priests, and crafty lawyers, slaves of us
    all have made ;
Our Emperor's grown a coward, our country's in
    the dust ;
Napoleon dare not draw the sword, it's covered all
    with rust."

Napoleon sat him silent, despairingly he smiled.
" I'll win them yet, I'll win them, these spirits
    fierce and wild !

Let's try the spell of kindness—the spell of measures
    mild,   .
I'll be patient and forbearing, and meek as little child.
I'll give them all they crave for, I'll make one more
    concess,
I'll give the boon long asked for—full liberty of press.
Like England let them bask in the sunshine of the
    press."

He gave—how did they use it?—the boon so wise
    withheld,
He knew they would abuse it; " No thanks ! " they
    loudly yelled.
All that's good and noble in the land it draggled in
    the mire,
And scorching words of hatred are writ in lines of
    fire.
Orleanists and angry Bourbons all filled with greed
    of power—
Even Thiers himself, that statesman old, in France's
    fatal hour.
" Nous sommes trahis ! nous sommes trahis ! " was
    the maddening mob's wild cry.
" Nous sommes trahis ! nous sommes trahis ! " the
    gamins make reply.

Thus hounded on and overwhelmed, an earthquake
  in his rear.
The tortured monarch sheds one bitter, sad, salt
  tear.
" Oh, Paris! giddy Paris! how fickle is thy smile!
Thou hast lured thy children onwards with Pleasure's fatal wile."

A lady lone sat waiting—she mourned her absent
  lord,
With courage unabating he'd drawn his rusting
  sword.
His pain-worn limbs were braced, his courage rose
  anew,
In Pleasure's hour unlaced, his harness on he drew.

Oh, many were the tears those beauteous eyes had
  shed,
As she worked the bright word " Glory! " in the
  gay and glancing thread.
" It shall flutter, noble lady, where France's bravest
  ·ride,
And my steel-clad files of Cuirassiers shall greet thy
  gift with pride,

When they see the silken banner flaunt bravely on
    their wing,

And echoing shouts of ' Vive la France!' shall
    make the welkin ring.

And if the worst betide me, why better gyve and
    rope,

Than life with Raspail for a King, Père Duchesne
    for a Pope.

Whatsoever fate befall me, I'll never lose my hope,

That brighter days will dawn for France, and
    France her eyes will ope.

And cheerfully I'll march to death, with bold un-
    swerving stride,

And Paris, blinded Paris, shall think of me with
    pride."

He turned his charger as he spake, '' Farewell for
    evermore ! ''

He gave his bridle reins a shake, " Adieu! adieu!
    once more."

He spurred his horse and rode away, though racked
    with ache and pain ;

He left the walls of Paris gay, ne'er to visit them
    again.

THE CZAR NICHOLAS.

THE CZAR NICHOLAS,

Russia teems with the materials out of which great minds are formed. Her vast Empire had long remained in the bonds of ignorance and barbarism:

> " Russia, and Russia's strength, lay long in darkest night;
> God said, ' Let Peter be,' and straightway there was light."

Russia has indeed been lucky alike in her rulers and the ruled. When we look back at what was accomplished by Peter the Great, Catherine, Nicholas, and last, but greatest of all, in his beneficent efforts for the happiness of his people, Alexander II., the present Emperor, we may indeed say, "There were giants in those days!" Every eye, bright with patriotism and enthusiasm, is now turned with admiration on the present Czar Alexander the Gentle. It was said of Cœur de Lion, and also of the great Earl of Warwick, the king-maker, " In him was valour and benevolence combined." So as Russia in her annals in former years had Peter the Great and Ivan the Terrible, so now, just as Italia in Victor Emmanuel has the

happiness of having her " Re Galantuomo," so
Russia will record in her future roll call of glorious
Czars, " Alexander the Gentle." He accomplished
the greatest work of all—the Emancipation of the
Serfs.

When we look at the awful cruelties and suffer-
ings, the ferocious hatreds and deadly hostility
which distinguished the sad internecine struggle
between the free Northern and the Southern slave-
holding states of the Great Republic, we are lost in
wonder that in an Empire so vast, a change so
sweeping, so grand, so utterly unexpected and
unhoped for by its millions, could possibly be
brought about with a perfect, utter, entire, complete
success, that we can only say, " the blessing of
God was on the work!" Under him we must
ascribe it to the unequalled and perfect docility of
the Russian people, their childlike love for the
Czar, their tacit obedience and respect for their
Government, their deep, all-pervading sense of
religion and fear of God.

The personal interest of the ruling and landown-
ing classes work clearly in direct antagonism to any
surrender of a single jot or iota of their privileges,
but they yielded them up to the amelioration of the
many.

While, however, we give to the lords of the soil
the full credit to which they are entitled for their
generosity and self-abnegation, we must give no

less credit to the masses. These latter found themselves suddenly, without preparation and without
being educated up to it, in a new-born state of
unfettered freedom. Very few nations would have
stood the test, but this northern nation, sunk as
they had been in the darkness of universal ignorance, suddenly emerged to occupy a situation equal
in its freedom to that of the most independent
Briton or American. In a calm and patient spirit
of the most perfect obedience to, and reliance
on, their Government and rulers, this immense
empire has been led onward through the various
grades of improvement up to a rational and per-
manent liberty.

TRANSLATIONS FROM THE RUSSIAN POETS.

To the student of history who observes and
closely analyses the rise and fall of nations and
peoples, nothing can be more interesting and de-
lightful than to mark the early dawn of literature
and intellect. Now that Russia has emerged from
her primeval state of chaos and barbarism into the
fierce light of progress and civilisation, it will be
a deeply interesting task to contrast the present
modern rich feasts of Slavonic literature, romance,
and poetry, with the earlier gems that appeared, few
and far between, like angel's visits, in her remoter
and darker ages. Russia now stands forth the
observed of all observers, with the eyes of the whole

civilized world upon her, as an object of the greatest
admiration and wonder. She is an instance of what
can be effected by what is described in our English
idiom, "a long pull, a strong pull, and a pull all
together." She has had the benefit of a few master
minds who have been filled with the spirit of devotion to their country, but the efforts of these master
minds would have been powerless if they had not been
seconded by the wonderful docility, and the loyal,
tractable spirit of the masses of the people. It is
difficult to realize how it was possible for the present
Czar to have effected such a wide, sweeping, and
entire reform as the emancipation of the serfs. We
must, however, give equal credit to the nobility,
gentry, and landowners, who cheerfully, graciously,
and ungrudgingly surrendered and gave up what
was to them almost life or death, the power of
owning souls. This was a privilege and institution
handed down to them and inherited from their
forefathers. All honour, therefore, be to them who
gave up such a privilege !

The war against Russia, commonly called the
Crimean War, was a war into which, as a statesman
truly said, " we drifted ; " the result, almost always,
of a feeble line of policy. The Manchester School,
as a body comprising many men of vast and compre-
hensive vision, having many ideas in themselves
sound, were hurried by the Extreme Left of the
party, and allowed some of the more zealous and

enthusiastic of their leaders to be their uncontrolled mouthpiece. Thus Cobden, great as he was in matters of commerce, which he understood, was quite at sea when he ventured into the unknown ocean of continental questions. On one occasion, in a violent speech in favour of Kossuth, whom he knew nothing about, he dared Russia to interfere in the civil war then raging between Austria and Hungary—a war, it may be added, which was solely one of nationalities and races. His words were, " We will crumple up Russia as I crumple up this bit of paper." If Cobden, always ready to admit he was wrong, were alive now, he would be the first to admit how much at random and off book he spake. Russia has shown herself not so easy to crumple up. When attacked by the united forces of Christendom and Mahommedanism she stood bravely at bay, and strong in the devoted attachment of the people to their Czar, their deep sense of religion, and patient, confiding submission to their Government, they showed a quiet, enduring power of resistance, and slow, plodding, dogged determination that could not fail to inspire their enemies with respect. Russia's rulers always select and endow with the highest rewards men who show capacity, and Todleben, of German extraction, well repaid such selection. Mouravieff, in spite of the tremendous call upon Russia's forces in the Crimea, was able to neutralize the glorious defence of Kars; and as the incompetency and want of foresight of the allied Generals neglected to march the Turkish contingent, lying idle and unemployed at Kertch and elsewhere, to its relief, it capitulated, and three of our best officers, Fenwick Williams, Lake, and Teesdale, were taken prisoners. Our generals could not see, that if they had only joined the army of Omar Pasha in relieving Kars they might then have easily obtained posses-sion of Tiflis and Georgia, roused the whole of Circassia, and struck a mortal blow at Russia in her most vital part. But as the Russian officers said, "Your eyes were smitten with blindness." Simi-larly after Alma, if the fleet had landed a few hun-dred blue-jackets and marines at the Bolbek, between Sebastopol and the heights of Alma, when the Russians fled into the town, a sudden attack inter-cepting them might have driven Menschikoff's army into the interior at once, and the allies might have entered the town thus open and unguarded from the land side. Todleben's genius at once saw how little we knew what we were about, and when it once came to a game of longbowls it simply became a question of which could pound longest and hardest. The attack at Inkerman was well planned, and ought to have succeeded. It failed in its details. The Russian army ought to have advanced much farther ere it deployed ; had they swept on in column right away to near Vernoutka, and made a feigned attack only at Inkerman, all the allied forces would have massed and concentrated at Inkerman, and the left wing of the Russians might have come down above Balaclava and shelled the shipping. Where should we have been then ?

Deep sleeping lay the Monarch,
  Deep sleeping lay the Czar ;
He dreamt of Holy Russia,
  He dreamt of glorious war.

Strength and valour lay reposing,
  In slumber deep unfeigned ;
On that stern and haughty forehead
  A calm profoundly reigned.

Yet on that calm unruffled brow,
  Indignant valour shone,
As he thought of foul profaneness
  In holy places done.

He raised him from his iron couch,
  He stretched his mighty arms,—
" Not for me the wine-cup sparkling,
  Not for me shine beauty's charms.

My daily task must onward,
    The task stern duty taught ;
Each morning sees some task begun,
    Each evening sees it wrought.

Shall Christian nations stand aloof,
    And stand in mute amaze,
As on Jerusalem's fair towers
    And ruined shrines they gaze ?

Shall Turk and Moslem dare pollute
    The sacred House of God ?
Shall turbaned Infidel dare tread
    Where holy footsteps trod ?

We've had enough of jargon ;
    Enough of chatter we ;
Diplomatists have done their work,
    The end we'll quickly see."

Through the gates the white Czar wandered,
Thus he mused, and sadly pondered,
        Musing on his destiny :—

" To put down mob and faction
With stern and ready action ;
To punish law's infraction ;
        This is my destiny.

Republican or Cossack,
  Europe must take her choice;
Order must be established,
  And stilled Rebellion's voice."

Then, like a wizard
  In his dark retreat,
He calls his spirits round him.
  Here 'twere meet
Record each hero skilled in warfare's game,
  Each wielding leader's staff:
· But 'twere too long to name.

Myriads of warriors, armed,
  Around like statues stand,
And stand in silence, mute,
  To wait his high command.

He scans with practised eye
  Their serried, stern array,
Like eagle soaring high
  That marks his distant prey.

Cossacks of Don and Ukraine,
  He rides their rank along;
" Zdrastriute, Batchiouka ! "
  They raise the Russ war-song.

Go proudly, horse, go proudly !
  Thou bearest Cæsar's weight ;
Thou carriest Hero Russ,
  Our Czar so stern and great.

His piercing eye beams proudly,
  He wears no waving plume,
His deep voice thunders loudly,
  Let none a word presume.

Army on army, in their proud array,
  Cover the snow-clad plains ;
Loud booms the cannon's roar,
  And hoarse artillery's strains.

"Look forth into the darkness,
  My Lagienka old ;
Look forth into the darkness,
  Some tidings must be told.

An end to dark forebodings,
  Forebodings dim and sad ;
Some tidings I must gather—
  Some tidings, good or bad."

" I go, my liege—I hasten :
    I'll spare nor whip nor spur !
Yet, hold ! I see a herald,
    But age my eyeballs blur.

I see a grey-haired veteran,
    He hither wends his way ;
He surely brings unto my liege
    Some tidings of the day."

The soldier stood erect and stiff,
    Saluting soldier-wise,
But ne'er a word escaped his lip,
    Salt tears stood in his eyes.

" What, ho ! what news, my Hetman old ?
    With ye how sped the day ?
Has fortune smiled upon our arms ?
    The news, come, quickly say.

Art dumb as well as deaf ? *
    I know thee, warrior true ;
Why standest thou then so silent ?
    And why so pale of hue ?

---

* General Sass, a venerable commander, had greatly distinguished himself in the mountain warfare against the Circassians. He was a great favourite with Paskiewitch, and was called " the Deaf General."

Come, tell thy tale full quickly,
　　And mind thou tell it true.
How fared the battle with thee ?
　　Which conquered, they or you ?

How fought these English mastiffs,
　　These bull-dogs fierce and rude ?
Have they my legions routed ?
　　Have they my arms withstood ?"

He raised unto his head his hand ;
　　His hand embrowned with toil.
His uniform was white with dust,
　　His boots all mud and soil.

" Come, quaff the ' Chaszta Zalatoi,'
　　Collect thy wits astray ;
Come sit thee down and slow recount
　　The tidings of the day."

He tasted not the proffered cup,
　　He panted for a word :
Deep sighs from broad breast struggled up ;
　　He touched his broken sword.

Impatiently the Romanoff
　　His servant watched awhile ;
He frowned and said, " Velikü Sass,
　　To see thee makes me smile.

Dost think thy monarch cannot face
　　Misfortune when it comes ?
Nay, comrade, take now heart of grace,
　　And think thou hear'st the drums."

He boldly faced his master,
　　He stared him in the face :
" I come to tell disaster,
　　No messenger of grace."

His tongue was loosed free,
　　His words flow quick apace :
" Let fools and cowards flatter thee,
　　The mightiest of thy race.

I'll tell the truth, though scorching
　　The bitter truth may be,
Our days of camps and marching
　　Our nights of agony.

I've come, my Czar, great Nicholas,
    I've come from rudest fray ;
Though bred to arms from childhood up
    I've ne'er seen such day.

I've quelled the proud Circassian
    As hunters quell the deer,
Revenge and hate's fierce passion
    Had banished ought like fear.

I've quelled the sons of Poland,
    The death-defying Hun,
But when we've beat these English
    The day's work's just begun.

They blench not, Sire, they blench not,
    These beef-devouring knaves !
Their courage cool odds quench not
    When battle fierce it raves.

They love the roar of battle,
    These stout ale-swilling churls !
They laugh at shell's shrill rattle
    As death around she hurls.

My liege, it boots not weary
　With details long thine ear,
As my sad tale unfolds it,
　The truth will soon appear.

Thine orders were obeyed,
No brigade was delayed ;
Your children were all ready,
No squadron was unsteady.

Before the holy altars
　Devoted all we bowed ;
Not one was coward, traitor,
　Among that countless crowd.

The Papes were at the altars,
　Confession all was told ;
They gave us absolution,
　We went forth free and bold.

They gave us of their cheer,
　Rye-bread and barley-beer ;
They gave us such strong ' Vodki,'
　It brought a scalding tear.

Säss, Rudiger, Liprandi,
  Marshalled that vast array ;
Of beef and strong corn-brandy,
  They stinted not that day.

We grasped our rifles firmly,
  We issued from the gate ;
The chalk cliffs looked down on us,
  For dawn we would not wait.

We cannot tell the reason
  That day it cost us dear,
But all we know is, beaten—
  Beaten we were, 'tis clear."

" Velikée Polko Vodets,
  Well hast thou earned thy due ;
Right well thy master values
  Servant so rough and true.

Nay ! never pipe thine eye, man,
  Thy shaggy eyelash wipe ;
Twist not thy mouth awry, man,
  Go home and smoke a pipe.

I love these deeds of daring,
   I love to hear you tell
How well my children bore themselves,
   My sturdy foes, how well.

Were all my orders carried out ?
   Was each man at his post ?
Were all my Hetmans ready
   To marshal forth my host?

Was any one there backward ?
   Did any stand aloof ?
Was any one a dastard,
   In coward's life behoof ? "

" Not one there shirked his duty,
   Not one was coward slave ;
Thy children were all worthy
   Of thee and comrades brave."

" I would," quoth grim old Nicholas,
   " That England's trusty sword
This day were doing battle
   For the saints and for the Lord.

What brings these sturdy Saxons,
 What brings our old allies,
To herd with bragging Gascons,
 And join their dark emprize ?

Shall eagles mate with buzzards ?
 Shall bisons fill a stall ?
To France's false usurper
 Shall England grovelling fall ? "

———————

Stretched on his bed of iron
 The dying monarch lay,
His thoughts still of his people
 Though fading fast away,

" God knows I love my subjects,
 Though oft I them oppress ;
I oft mistake and injure
 When I full fain would bless.

My courtiers all delude me,
 The truth I cannot find ;
Oh ! who would be a monarch,
 And lose his peace of mind ?

I fain would live in concord
    With nations near and far,
For State-craft and for safety
    Perforce compelled to war."

In that hour of deep contrition,
Clearer lights stole o'er his vision,
And his last thought, manumission,
    Unto serf and thrall to bear.

A legacy he left his heirs,
Bequeathed to him by his forbears,
To free each serf and bonded thrall,
And make them freemen one and all.

A legacy to loose, unbind,
Freedom of thought, and will, and mind;
Each loosed, free, unfettered thrall,
Shall blessings on his monarch call ;
And freeborn sons their Czar shall hail,
Who listened kind to serfdom's wail.
This done, his spirit soar'd away—
That giant form now senseless clay.

SUNSET OF THE NINETEENTH CENTURY.

SUNSET OF THE NINETEENTH CENTURY.
The Eastern Question;
Meeting of the Three Great Monarchs.

A state of great uncertainty and disquietude has now existed for nearly two years, misgivings, vague, mystic, unaccountable, haunt the minds of all. Trade and commerce have been and still remain hampered and paralysed; doubt and suspicion reign universally on the Continent—the tide of emigration sweeping off the flower of the manhood and bone and sinew of the Continent; strikes and union, disunion among all the workmen in all' branches of industries; labour raising its suicidal and fratricidal hand against capital; glutted markets, occasioned by excess of production; "men's hearts failing them for very fear." It was while the thoughts of all Europe were disquieted, and the Statesmen and ruling authorities of the Great Powers looked strangely on each other, that the Three Great Potentates, who, for the time, were most concerned, resolved to meet together and see if they could not put an end to this state of doubt and uncertainty, of suspicion and mistrust. Those who can read between the lines know that the Three Emperors had no

arrière pensées, no selfish or unworthy motives.
Peace to all three was and is a vital necessity, but,
as to the best means of promoting that object there
could not but be varied and divers views and
opinions.   The trials of the reckless adventurers
who had destroyed all that twenty years of peace
and prosperity had raised up in Paris, and the open
and boastful admissions of the Delegates and Chiefs
of the Commune had revealed the fact of a vast
organization of revolutionists and socialists, who
merged all patriotism and indeed any other sentiment
common to mankind in the one enterprize to which
they had sworn to devote themselves, body and soul,
heart and hand, viz. : the destruction and uprooting
of all society.   The Czar of Russia was only too
well aware that his vast Empire was honeycombed
with secret societies : he knew the terrible danger
that lay behind if a popular and taking cry was once
raised by the Socialists which would chime in with
the ultra-patriotic and Chauvinist and Pan-Sclavistic
ideas of the old Russian or national party,
combined with the Omladines.   All countries of
course have or ought to have enthusiastic ideas of
patriotism, and an ardent desire to see their country
increase in power and greatness ; but the danger
always lies in the impatience of the people to bide
their time, and their too willing attention to the
voices of wild and impulsive enthusiasts.   The Czar
foresaw that if he did not get his brother Emperors

to stand on the engine of State with him, to help him to apply the brake, the passengers themselves would force the Stoker to pile on the fuel and sit on the safety valve until a rate of speed was attained that must end in some tremendous catastrophe. The meeting was a wise and prudent step, conceived in the best interests of all their people, as long as Austrian Hungary, through Andrassy, would rely on Bismark and Germany, and take no action without their consent and approval, any attempt at aggressive policy forced on the Czar by the old Russian party, insidiously led on by the secret societies who had raised the cry of Pan-Slavism, would be neutralized by the calm but determined attitude of that Power which held the key of the Balkans.

> Say where shall peace affrighted
>   A safe asylum find ?
> Our souls with fears are blighted,
>   The nations all are blind !
>
> Uprose the genius of the Rhine*
>   Majestic from her throne,
> " Why trouble ye my waters ?
>   My fountains leave alone.

---

* There has always been a tradition that a Spirit of the House, the " White Lady of Potsdam," is always seen before any great event.

Rumours of wars are vexing
 The spirit of my flood,
The calmness of my current
 Is chafed like rushing blood.

Germania mourns her commerce,
 Her pining Industry,
Untilled her fields, her hardy sons
 Across th' Atlantic flee.

I'll get me to the Kaiser
 I'll seek him in his halls,
I'll pray him rise and stretch forth
 His hand to stop these brawls;

These brawls and broils, unworthy
 Of Christian nations free,
Got up by scheming placemen
 And trickster's gramarye ! "

The Kaiser sat all lonely,
 Untasted stood the wine,
" I feel me old and weary,
 For peace and rest I pine."

The spirit of the waters
   Stood, lo ! within the hall.
" Kaiser ! in thought thou'st summoned me
   I answer to thy call.

" Why call'st thou me ! why leaving
   My cool sequestered cave,
Am I borne upward headlong
   To breast the boisterous wave ?

" The sound of many waters,
   Is thundering in mine ear.
Woe's me ! the sound of cannon
   And tumbril's roll I hear."

" Sweet spirit ! give me comfort,
   White lady tell me how
To still these jarring tumults,
   Our heads they earthward bow."

" Pour oil upon my waters
   Go seek thy brothers true,
No more of wars and slaughters,
   The skies shall soon be blue !

" Spirit of strength, I'll go forth,
   Thou beckonest with thy hand
I'll seek my brother Kaiser,
   Far in the cold North Land.

" He's lonely in his greatness,
   He yearns for love and truth,
As age draws on, he misses
   The friends of early youth.

" I'll seek my brother Kaiser,
   By Danube's water blue,
I'll seek my younger brother,
   The brave, the bold, the true.

" Sweet peace, we three will guard thee,
   Unto each other true,
And he that dare offend thee,
   Shall it right deeply rue."

GLADSTONE AT DUNROBIN.

GLADSTONE AT DUNROBIN.

Dunrobin's halls are crowded,
　With lairds and ladies gay,
Diplomatists and statesmen
　A varied, mixed array.

Professors scientific,
　And all who worship art ;
Writers, of brain prolific,
　Each acts his varied part.

Why stands yon man so lonely,
　His thoughts are far away
Unmindful he of music's strains,
　Southward they wandering stray.

With lofty brow, and massive jaw,
　Clasped as with iron band,
Distinguished by his noble port
　His looks of stern command.

He stands apart secluded,
  And lonely from the rest,
Vast schemes of Reformation,
  Swell high within his breast,

His heart is in the Senate,
  His heart it is not here,
He cares not for the Highlands,
  He cares not for the deer.

He cares not for the dun deer,
  He cares not for the roe,
His heart is in the Senate,
  Wherever he may go!

The salmon leaps unheeded,
  Unheeded leaps the roe.
The State his service needed,
  And southwards he must go.

On that pale brow is lowering,
  A dark and heavy frown,
Genius has on him set her seal,
  And marked him for her own.

Those earnest eyes are flashing,
　From them his soul looks out,
Fierce indignation lashes,
　All foes he'll put to rout.

Foul jobs and foul abuses,
　Old wrongs long unredressed,
Reforms long meditated,
　Classes and trades oppressed.

" How long shall foul and noxious weeds
　England's fair garden fill ?
How rank they grow, and choke the ground
　That honest men should till !

" The prunning knife is wanted sore,
　These rotten twigs to shear,
When axe and bill have done their work,
　The sun shall enter here.

" Old England's oak shall bloom again,
　Her boughs shall heavenwards soar,
Fresh light into her shades I'll let
　Her wasted strength restore.

" Lopped of her useless branches,
   From foul excrescence free,
Green with new sap and vigorous
   Shall tower that stately tree ! "

*   *   *   *   *   *   *

Two years of headlong progress,
   Two stirring years have flown,
And Samson Agonistes
   Still sternly holds his own !

He, sick at heart, and ill at ease,
   A smile must ever wear ;
Each backer shy must try to please ;
   Such smiling costs him dear.

His spirit high, and nature proud,
   He now must rein and school,
And honied words the scorn enshroud
   He feels for noisy fool.

A bold, unflinching front present
   To friends and foes alike ;
With soothing syrup rows prevent,
   Yet still prepared to strike.

One night the world seemed hateful :
    All hopeless seemed the strife ;
Fawcett and James, ungrateful,
    A burden made his life.

"Intransigentes," White-boys,
    Home Rulers, Rods and Roughs,
They wrangled, with no slight noise,
    They dealt each other cuffs.

He heard them, but he heeded not,
    He cared not for their howls :
Their sympathy he needed not,
    He valued less their growls.

The tailors ten of Tooley Street,
    And all that rabble rout,
With muttered curses loud and deep,
    Demand why they're left out.

Full fain they'd gain an entrance ;
    Full fain they'd ope the door,
But Bright's broad back is guarding it,
    And none shall tread that floor.

With burly back against the door,
    He kept intruders out,
He guarded well that sacred floor,
    From vile and rabble rout!

All honor to thee, glorious John!
    Thou'st served thy country well!
What various ills thou'st saved her from?
    What evils, who can tell?

*   *   *   *   *   *   *

He sought his study, weary,
    Where classic tomes invite;
The coal fire burned so cheery,
    He sought a short respite.

From days of toil expended,
    And nights of little ease,
With every nerve distended,
    The madding mob to please.

He sought his study, weary,
    That study seemed a bore,
And yet how bright and cheery
    That study seemed of yore.

" Shall scholar wise and sage severe
    With swine and snobs consort ?
Who none my lettered lore revere,
    Of base and sordid heart ? "

He flung him in his arm-chair,
    Disgusted, sick at heart.
" Some comfort here, none over there,
    I'll play no more the part."

He nodded at old Homer,
    Whose bust on bracket stood :
" Methinks to read a chapter
    Perchance would do me good."

He reached him down an Iliad,
    To pass away the time,
It soothed him like an opiad,
    The slow and measured rhyme.

He slept, and in his slumber
    He heard a heavenly strain ;
The Muses, nine in number,
    Seek their lost child again.

" O renegade ! return ;
  We mourn thy absence long ;
Why thus thine early playmates spurn,
  Thou child of classic song ? "

The shade of Homer rises !
  An old man crowned with bay,
His sightless eyes reproachful,
  A mute rebuke convey.

" Thou'st served thy country long enough,
  Deservest well repose ;
England has need of coarser stuff,
  To meet her coming woes.

" Thine earnest mood is chafed sore
  At aught like jest or jeer,
'Tis fitted not for faction's roar,
  Or party's selfish sneer ! "

He slept, but soon a change came o'er
  The spirit of his dreams ;
With axe in hand he stood, and now
  A woodman strong he seems.

'Tis merry, 'tis merry, in good greenwood,
   The birds are gaily singing ;
On the beech's pride and the brown oak's side
   Sir William's axe is ringing.

No more the Pines, the grand old Pines,
   The tall, the stately Pine,
Whose giant girths the Ivy bines
   With loving clasp entwine.

Their prostrate trunks all shivered,
   Torn down their leafy screen ;
How sweet the sun once glimmered
   Soft through their foliage green.

These were thy charms, sweet woodland,
   But all thy charms have fled,
Thy pleasant glades have vanished,
   And all thy charms are dead.

The Dryads shriek, " Whose ruthless hand
   Hath wrought this cruel wrong ?
At whose audacious rash command
   Fall down these giants strong ? "

" How dear these woodlands once to me,
　　The ring-dove coo'd and murmured there,
The squirrel leaped from tree to tree,
　　And all was peace and liberty.

No more shall squirrel shell his nuts,
　　And gambol full of glee ;
Woodpeckers green no more shall tap
　　At hollow beechen tree.

No more shall glossy creepers
　　And tender ivy-bine
Their rugged sides encircle,
　　Their gnarled girth entwine.

The oak that in summer was pleasant to hear,
And rustled its leaves at the fall of the year,
Is gone !　In its place no sapling is grown.

Piping breeze no more shall greet it,
Bowing branch no more shall meet it ;
'Tis gone ! and its site all unmarked and unknown.

Uprose the demon of the wild,
  The genius of the hill;
It was the fairy elfin king,
  His voice was weird and shrill.

" Why sounds yon stroke on beech and oak,
  Frighting my foliage green ?
And who goes there that doth so dare
  Molest my leafy screen ?

" Ruin seize thee, ruthless wretch !
  Confusion on thy councils wait !
May traitor turn each former friend,
  Like thee, O base ingrate !

" Kehama's curse, may 't cling to thee—
  The curse of sleepless eyes ;
The curse that haunts the traitor's breast,
  The worm that never dies."

He woke ! a chilly shiver
  Came o'er him as he lay ;
His blood ran cold, like river,
  All icy bound, or clay.

" Have I done wrong ? " he muttered ;
　" Is it too late to mend ? "
An anguished prayer he uttered,
　That all might be at end.

　　*　　*　　*　　*　　*　　*

He woke, and turned uneasily,
　The scene it shifts once more ;
Th' Atlantic's freshening breezily
　On emerald Erin's shore.

A bow-shot off a ruin stands,
　An ivy-mantled porch ;
Belfry lies low among the sands,
　Like quench'd funereal torch.

Who comes, with calm, sad, kindly face,
　Reproachful in his look ;
" This is thy work, this is no place,
　Thou who thy vengeance took."

" Go home, go home," the pale man said,
　" This is no place for thee ;
Art come to triumph o'er the dead,
　Thy wicked work to see."

"Thou'st quench'd five hundred household fires,
  See that thine own burn bright ;
Cold are the hearths of hundred homes,
  Robbed of their warmth and light."

Abashed he stood, when lo ! a priest,
  In priestly cassock clad ;
" 'Twas done for thee, and thou at least
  Say, if my work be bad ? "

" It was not done for us," he cried,
  "But for thine own sweet will ;
It ministered unto thy pride,
  And thou art Jesuit still."

" I love my brother, here's his home,
  " With me a warm welcome ;
Like brothers we'll together roam,
  And muse o'er classic tome."

" In friendly true fidelity
  We will our notes compare :
For he was raised at Trinity,
  And I at Saint Omer."*

* St. Omer used to be the great Classical College for
Catholic Priests.

Return, then, son of Isis,
    'Erst " Alma Mater's " pride,
Shake off thy only vices,
    The sins of wounded pride.

" Then, woodman, spare this tree,
    Touch not a single bough ;
In youth it sheltered me,
    And I'll protect it now ! "

The church still left, O woodman,
    Relentless, pause awhile ;
Touch not her branches, rude man,
    Heed not the tempter vile.

He woke, a prayer he uttered,
    Straight vanished all his pride ;
" Perhaps I'm wrong," he muttered,
    " The country shall decide."

Despair then on his soul took place,
    When, lo ! a vision, fair ;
His Catherine's sweetly smiling face
    Shows radiant by his chair !

"Be of good cheer, my lord," she said,
  "For all regrets are vain ;
May blessings shower upon thy head,
  And make thee young again ! "

"Thou'st need of rest, and change of scene,
  A well-earned, long repose ;
Thou soon will wear a front serene,
  Forgiving all thy foes."

"Sweet Catherine, we will take the train,
  And put our heads for Mald ;
How Gladstone is 'himself again,'
  The tale shall soon be told.

"And while the muses I invite,
  O'er Schlieman's triumphs pore,
To poor and needy thou'lt attend,
  I to my classic lore."

"While thou, my love, art at my side,
  My children at my knee,
How gladly will our galley glide
  On Clwydd's* glassy sea."

* The Clwydd and the Elwy form an Estuary near the
ancient City of Rhuddllan.

" How fair thou art to-day," he prest
    Her hand, "though always fair,   ·
Ill dreams no more disturb my rest,
    If thou art only there."

A knock! and lo! there enters there
    A well-known, friendly face ;
He takes the proffered easy chair,
    As 'twere his 'customed place.

"Envy not me," the statesman cried,
    " For unto thee is left,
That which of all in life I prized,
    Of that now I'm bereft.

" The blessed partner of my life,
    With many virtues rife,
The healing balm of party strife,
    A fond and faithful wife."

Then held he out a friendly hand,
    Though tears streamed down his face ;
Behold, in great forgiveness grand,
    These rivals twain embrace.

Then, arm-in-arm, adown the street,
Adown Pall Mall they strode;
They held both, as 'twas only meet,
Sweet converse by the road.

Amazed, the House beheld that sight,
And wondering, rubbed their eyes;
Their eyes could not believe aright,
'Twas far too great surprise.

How smiled the angels down from heaven,
To see the work was done;
Pride thus perished, love thus conquered,
And avenged God's murdered son.

THE GOOD SHIP "PROGRESS."

THE GOOD SHIP "PROGRESS."

Two years of progress rapid,
  Two years had quickly flown ;
How flat, and stale, and vapid,
  His triumphs now have grown.

A greedy, grasping crowd,
  His ante-chamber fill ;
Demand, with clamour loud,
  A share of treasury till.

Time-serving trimmers, all
  Base worshippers of pelf :
For place and power they brawl,
  Their thoughts still all for self.

(PASSENGERS BEGIN TO GET SEA-SICK.)

O Gladstone, prithee, pause awhile,
  O do but give us rest ;
For change, reform and progress,
  We all have lost our zest.

We've had enough of action,
    And enough of motion we ;
Rolled to starboard, rolled to larboard,
    While the waves are surging free.

We are all very giddy,
    Our legs and knees they shake,
Our hearts they fail within us,
    Our inmost souls do quake.

O save us father Dizzy,
    And only take us home ;
On " terra firma " place us,
    We will no longer roam.

Go call brave Ben, the bo'sun,
    It is our only chance ;
If aught remain to save us,
    He'll see it at a glance.

Then run and wake up Dizzy,
    He must be tired of bed ;
He's never drunk or fizzy ;
    Shout till you wake the dead.

Ben rubbed his eyes, and grumbled,
  "What's up now," thereupon
Straight out of bed he tumbled,
  And put his breeches on.

" Bout ship, lets beat to windward,
  And weather, if we can ;
Lee shore and breakers roaring,
  She ne'er such danger ran."

" Steady, steer small, and mind your helm,
  My hearties, cheerily .
We'll right the vessel of the realm,
  Though lab'ring wearily."

How jocund sounds his whistle shrill,
  The silver bo'sun's call ;
With cheerful face, so calm and still,
  He cheers them one and all.

Start tacks and sheets, the halyards free,
  The bellying mainsail stay,
Haul aft and home, the helm's a-lee,
  Belay ! my boys, belay !

She forges on, gains steerage way,
   Her sails they gaily fill;
"D——d near in irons," the bo'sun said,
   "Not into port, though, still."

Sweethearts and wives we soon will toast,
   Our grog we soon will sip;
The Rads no more shall rule the roast,
   Keep a stiff upper lip.

*   *   *   *   *   *   *

Our ancient institutions,
   And our grand old British laws,
Our altar, throne, our hearth and home,
   In such a righteous cause.

O his must be a coward heart
   That would not lift a hand,
For children, wives, for free born lives,
   And such a native land.

JOHN BRIGHT—SALMON FISHING IN SUTHERLAND.

JOHN BRIGHT—SALMON FISHING IN SUTHERLAND.

Nothing can be a greater proof of the rapid strides of civilization than the wonderful change which has come over the more remote Highlands of Scotland. Five-and-twenty years ago, as a boy at College, I used to go up (by coach the whole way) to shoot grouse and deer in Sutherlandshire. At that time sheep farming had only just begun. The whole country had been entirely in the hands of a few poverty-stricken Celtic populations, who never did a day's work from one year's end to the other, and passed their time entirely in spearing "black" salmon out of season, and full of spawn, thus destroying millions of fish, while the fish so captured was unwholesome, if not pernicious. When they could not do this, they killed the poor hinds big with young, because at that time they could be easily approached, while the stags were sucking and their flesh rank and nauseous. The then Duchess of Sutherland tried all she could to induce these people to emigrate. She offered them free passes

to grants of land in Canada. Having tried per-
suasion in vain, she was at length induced by her
factors (or agents) to take stronger measures, and
evict them. They were most amply and generously
provided for, and now form a happy and contented
population in Canada, occupying several townships.
Their place was taken by shrewd, canny, Lowland
shepherds, who walked up from the Lammermuirs,
and were backed by the Scottish Joint Stock Banks.
These new tenants introduced the system of
"smearing," or, in other words, waterproofing
the Lowland whitefaced, Cheviot sheep. This pro-
cess enables the sheep to withstand the rigours of
that hyperborean climate. With the Lowlanders
and their sheep, came also canny Lowland habits
of industry and thrift; and from a howling wilderness, where only the crow of the grouse and the
bellowing of the stag were heard, there soon re-
sounded the whiz of the threshing machine and the
hum of the steam engine. Instead of the eggs of
the grouse being trod on, the kipper and milter
being killed out of season, and the hind big with
young murdered, there is a smiling population of
shepherds and sheep-farmers, while the county
yields a fine rent-roll to its owner, and everybody
is benefited. Nevertheless, the Duchess, the late
Duke, and all his factors and agents, were met with
the most bitter hostility and violent abuse. The
poachers and illicit whiskey, or "sma' still" -

smugglers, met with champions in all the professional agitators and demagogues of the day.
The *Times* itself sent a commissioner to inquire into
the alleged wrongs of the evicted tenants and
so-called martyrs. We believe the commissioner
went back satisfied that a great good had been
brought about; but the early impressions of the
Times, no doubt, had been warped, by the reckless
assertions and bare allegations, unsupported by
proof, of professional agitators, and the hotheaded
zealots who are their tools. It was while occupying
one of these farms that the writer had frequent
opportunities of seeing Mr. Bright pursuing his
sport by pool or stream, and also noticed Mr. Gladstone rambling among the wild and romantic scenery
of the beautiful County of Sutherland. The Dowager
Duchess, as gifted in mind as she was charming in
face and feature, delighted to collect together at
Dunrobin Castle, all who were distinguished by
intellect and attainments, whether in politics, war,
science, art, or music. There might be seen Sir
Edwin Landseer, Sir Roderick Murchison, Mrs.
Beecher Stowe, ("Uncle Tom's Cabin"); and others,
rubbing shoulders with Lord Lansdowne, Lord
Aberdeen, Mr. Sydney Herbert, and all the great
politicians and diplomatists of the age. Within
that charmed circle of born and hereditary aristocracy were welcomed all comers who bore the
stamp of the aristocracy of genius and intellect.

No other card of admission was required. At Dunrobin the great rising statesman, Gladstone, first met John Bright, " the great tribune," and representative of the " Manchester School." There was formed the great coalition, which certainly brought great changes. The future will reveal their results.

Brightly, briskly flows the Brora,*
    From her home mid mountain snows,
Past boulders huge and granite blocks,
    That would her course oppose.

Shin and Oykel's* blended waters
    Swift hurry to the sea,
Where " Suter's "† cliffs o'er arching,
    Guard the shores of Cromarty.

Northwards all down the Naver,*
    Where winds blow keen and hoar,
Where birch-trees gently waver,
    Along the silver shore.

---

* Three of the most noted salmon streams in Sutherland. Naver is Norwegian or Scandinavian for the Birch. These coasts, as well as that of Caithness, were colonized by Scandinavian Settlers.

† " Suters," and the Cobbler, two lofty cliffs at Bay of Cromarty.

A burly form in fisher's garb,
　　The gentle art pursues,
He trims his Kirby hooks * keen barb,
　　With gaudy pheasant's hues.

With hackle brown and peacock's harl
　　He decks the tinsel lure,
To tempt the monarch of the flood
　　From watery caves secure.

" Mag in her braws," the " butcher," †
　　All clad in colours gay,
Of golden pheasant feathers,
　　Of partridge, grouse, and jay.

Glancing with fairy glamour,
　　They offer tempting lure,
Like maid whom gods enamour,
　　They'll tempt the prey, be sure.

He waves aloft a mighty wand,
　　While on the waters brown
His line wide circling round his head
　　He drops like thistle down !

---

* The best form of Hook is " Kirby Bend."
† Two noted and deadly Salmon Flies.

A tug—a pull—a gurgling swell,
   Some monster from below,
He feels the cruel steel, he darts
   Like arrow from the bow!

Swift from the reel through rattling rings,
   The line runs cheerily,
He feels the butt, his side upturns,
   All spent and wearily.

Wind up thy line, unscrew thy rod,
   Thy task is o'er, John Bright,
'Tis time for thee to homeward plod,
   E'er fades the autumn light.

MISCELLANEOUS.

SCHWERT-LIED—"THE SONG OF THE SWORD."

SCHWERT-LIED—"THE SONG OF THE SWORD."

Translation from Körner.*

" Why gleams thy blade so blue ? "
" Dost ask, thou warrior true,
Why gleams my blade so blue ? "
" I hear the battle from afar,

                  Hurrah !

"I love to hear it swell—
I know the sound so well ! "
" Why rings thy blade within
Thy sheath with jar and din,
Thou fiercely clanging blade ? "
                  Hurrah !

---

* Theoder Körner was a cavalry officer. He was the *beau idéal* of a soldier-poet. He was the German Dibdin, and our sailors were not more familiar with their favourite " Tom Bowling," and " Will Watch the Bold Smuggler," than is every German soldier with " Morgen Roth " and " Mein

" Dost ask my sheath within
Why leap with such a din ?
I hear the cannon's voice—
This makes my heart rejoice.
War ! war ! my life's best choice—
This makes me leap within.

Hurrah !

" No longer by my side,
Like coy and blushing bride,
Thy timid glances hide ;
Head pillowed on my breast,
Take now thy well-earned rest.

Hurrah !

Schwert." When German troops are on a long march and
begin to get leg-weary, the colonel calls for the best singer
with the best voice, and he trolls forth one of their well-known
songs. As the men join in the chorus, fatigue, and hunger,
and hardship are all forgotten, and they sing their weariness
away. Nothing can be more solemn and impressive than to
hear a huge Cuirassier or stalwart Fusilier send forth from his
deep, broad chest, the guttural notes and swelling words of
one of those German war-hymns of Körners. As the whole
troop join in the chorus their thoughts are elevated, and the
beautiful words of the song go home to them, and all home
feelings and love of Fatherland swell within their breasts.
Then, all of a sudden, the note is changed, and another voice
joins in with some lilting love-song to a lively air ; then they

" My bride ! my iron bride !
I hear the squadrons dash,
I hear the mitraille crash,
I see the sabres flash.

> Hurrah !

" I hear the bursting shells.
Ring out, ye marriage bells !
Hark ! to the sound that tells
Of dying warriors' knells.
That gruesome revelry."

> Hurrah !

break into a quick step, or shake their jaded horses into a
trot, and they realise the old English melody :—

> " Jog on, jog on, the foot-path way,
> So merrily mount the stile a' ;
> Your merry heart goes a' the day.
> Your sad one tires in a mile a'."

Körner's soldiers' songs, or rather battle-hymns, all breathe
forth a deep sense of religion. He possessed the true hero
soul of the old Berserker, inspired with love of war and song.
In his chivalrous and lofty spirit of devotion to his country he
resembled John Grahame of Claverhouse : the same chiselled
beauty of feature, such as ladies love to look upon ; their hopes
and aspirations were the same ; both expressed the dearest
wish of their hearts, " to die on some well-fought field, their
last word ' Forward !' their last breath a cheer." Their
wishes were granted ; both died shot through the heart in the
moment of victory !

SOLDATEN-LIED MORGEN ROTH.

K

SOLDATEN-LIED—" MORGEN ROTH.'

Translation from Körner.*

Sunny Morn, with hues so red,
Soon I'll number 'mong the dead;
When thy early beams arise,
I shall be beyond the skies.

Youth and Beauty, what are they?
Creatures of a short-lived day;
Cherry cheek and laughing eye,
Sweet they are—how soon they die.

What is Life? 'tis but a span.
What is poor, vain, sinful man?
Toil and trouble, trouble, toil,
Carking care, and sad turmoil.

' See note on p. 125.

Only yestern I was prancing
On my war-steed, pennons glancing :
Now shot through the heart, I die,
In the cool grave soon I lie.

Happen then whatever may,
Let it come in God's own way ;
I am ready, ready still,
Still prepared to do His will.
If I live, or if I die,
God is with me, ever nigh.

Scarcely tasted is life's cup,
'Ere we're called to give it up ;
Soon the round of pleasure's game
Ends in sorrow, sin, and shame.

I shall need no pall or bier ;
O'er me, comrades, drop a tear ;
Give me, for a soldier meet,
Soldier's cloak for winding sheet.

To Him, if me God shall call,
Foremost fighting I will fall ;
With my face turned to the foe,
Upwards to the stars I'll go.

Carve no line and rear no stone,
Leave, oh ! leave me quite alone ;
Only say when I am gone,
Only to my parents tell,
" He hath done his duty well :
True he was in heart and mind,
He leaves no bolder heart behind ; "

Earth ! how fade the hopes we borrow !
E'en thy days are nought but sorrow ;
Fleeting is thy beauty's glow,
Vain deceit, and empty show.

ANGRY THOUGHTS.

ANGRY THOUGHTS.

(TRANSLATED FROM THE RUSSIAN OF LOMONOSOV.)

ANGRY thoughts, when first they rise,
　Flashing from the angry eyes,
Easy 'tis the link to sever,
　Quick! dissolve the chain for ever.

Angry words ! O let them never
　Take a form, assume a shape,
While 'tis time arise, e'er ever,
　From thy lips a word escape !

Angry looks ! a savage frown,
　Scowling brow, and mouth drawn down,
Smiling cheek, and laughing eye
　Vanish, friends affrighted fly !

Angry looks ! what foul distortion,
　Feature, form, and face disguise !
Methinks this must be some abortion
　Monstrous, foul inhumanize.

Methinks some spirit from the sky
　Has done our fellow creature wrong,
Alike his mien and bearing changed,
　A prey to passions strong.

Angry deeds! thus Cain 'gainst Abel,
　Lifted once his impious hand,
And in fury, fratricidal,
　Brother's blood bestrew the strand.

Angry thoughts! 'ere once outspoken,
　Into thin air soon dissolve,
Soon the thread of thought is broken,
　Better feelings soon prevail.

Angry thoughts! in fatal hour,
　'Ere they take a spoken form,
Hence, thou dread and hideous power,
　Tender Conscience take alarm!

Angry thoughts! 'tis time for Prayer,
　To thy chamber quick repair!
Haste thee! quickly shut the door!
　Humbly kneel and press the floor!

On thy knees in fear remain,
  Rise not, faint not, struggle still,
Soon a gracious ear thou'lt gain,
  Calmly wait awhile God's will !

Hush ! for shadowy forms are near,
  Soft they whisper in thine ear,
Blessings and rebukes bestow,
  Spirit forms are here below.

See ! in streams of light descending,
  Spirit forms are hovering near,
Ministering angels tending
  All they loved and cared for here !

Victory ! now the conflict's o'er
  Quickly rise and ope the door,
Let thy thoughts now heavenward soar,
  Tempter hence, and tempt no more !

CHARGE OF THE
WHITE CUIRASSIERS AT
GRAVELOTTE.

CHARGE OF THE WHITE CUIRASSIERS AT GRAVELOTTE.

They called us " Slow Teutons " they dubbed us
   " Our Foes,"
Professors and pedants with spectacled nose,
To munch " sauer kraut," and to quaff sour wine,
And to smoke our big pipes on the banks of the
   Rhine.

That slander has melted like snow in the sun,
   It dims not the tombs where our brothers repose ;
On many a mitrailleuse, mortar and gun,
   Its denial is writ in the blood of our foes.

'Twas hopeless ! and yet in their soul's lofty daring,
   As he waved his bright falchion aloft o'er his head,
Not one gave a thought that the mandate was bearing
   Himself and his comrades to die midst the dead.

'Twas desperate ! 'twas hopeless ! yet onwards they
    bounded,
With the speed of the whirlwind, at word of com-
    mand ;
With Kaiser's onlooking, by legions surrounded,
    They slacked not their onset, that Patriot Band !

The *mêlée* is over ! woe ! woe ! for the number
    Of saddles all empty ! the muster-roll call !
No " Bott sell " * shall rouse them again from their
    slumber,
And nought is left for us save to weep at their fall !

And the might of Napoleon down smote by the
    sword,
Hath melted like snow at the glance of the Lord ;
Zouaves and Spahis, 'tis a race for dear life,
Which shall first quit the field and escape from the
    strife.

The braggarts and bullies of Paris gay town
Henceforward shall tremble and pale when we frown.
" Leave alone the stern Teuton—of him let's be shy ;
Let's mind our own business ! " henceforward the cry.

---

* " Bott Sell " is a bugle call, the same as our sounding
" Boot and Saddle."

IRISH SOLDIERS.

IRISH SOLDIERS.

NOTHING can be more ill advised than ever interfering with the Irish when the whiskey is in them. They make the best soldiers in the world, but the iron band of discipline needs at certain times and seasons the relaxation coveted by our human nature.

"Ne que semper arcum tendit Apollo."

At these times, when they are on the war path, popularly known here as "on the spree," or, as they call it in Australia, "on the burst," the great thing is for the sergeants and non-commissioned officers to keep carefully away from them; their own sweethearts and lasses and people will manage them and soothe them with a "Take it aisy now, Pat, good luck to you, take it fair and aisy," and if their uproariousness and violence passes all bounds, they will give them a gentle but ceremonious hiding, and tumble them on to a bed, where they will soon sleep off the liquor, and, without any harm being done, they will return to their colors and their duty better soldiers than ever, and remain so until the time arrives in its proper season when "a bust" is due. The fact is, an Irishman is such a splendid specimen of humanity that his high spirits and physical health require a safety valve to let off the superfluous steam. To use his own rich doric, he "gets blue

moulded for want of a bating." The right hand of
my company in the S—— M—— was an Irish
navvy, Matthew Finnigan. He was a County
Tipperary man, and with his brother Jack had
passed a sort of college finishing as a navvy in the
black country. If managed, he was a splendid
soldier, standing some six feet five inches. He was
always obedient and docile, till one unfortunate
Saturday (market day at S——y) he brought a
candidate for the line into which I was then
enlisting recruits at the rate of £4 per man. I of
course ought to have invested it in the savings'
bank in his name, and I knew I was doing wrong at
the time, but I feared lest the man should think I
was committing a breach of faith and not keeping
my word, and as the money was his own to do what
he liked with, I politely handed it over. The result
may be guessed; the dram shops soon made him
what I dare say he would call " quite comfortable,"
but it was very uncomfortable for everybody else,
as his notion of comfort was to clear the town,
which he speedily did ; and as the stupid sergeants
would not leave him alone, he finished by getting
a blow from the steel end of a pair of handcuffs,
which a plucky but too zealous sergeant gave him
on the forehead. He was carried off to the infir-
mary, where, after two days and nights of insensi-
bility he woke up, stared round him, simply uttering
the words, " Thank God I am an Irishman."

ON BARMAIDS.

ON BARMAIDS.

No class is more misjudged and misinterpreted
than the "neat handed Phillis" who serves out
to her customers the good creatures of this life.
Many misjudge her winning ways and captivating
charms. The poor lasses come up from the country
having heard from their friends and neighbours
how their schoolfellow, Polly Hopkins, had married
a gentleman, and how Susy Simpson had become
the wife of the landlord of the hotel where she was
the barmaid. All honour be to the landlord who
chose a wife from among those who had served him
well and faithfully—he chose wisely. Let every
one honour him and take their hats off to him,
and let no one dare to presume to say, "He
has lowered himself—he married his barmaid." He
has done nothing of the sort. In raising her to the
level of his own position, he has raised both ! He
has set a good example, and she is a shining beacon
to other girls of the same class, that though their
duties may be hard, and onerous, and monotonous,
with "long days of lengthening labour and nights

of little ease," strict attention to their duties, and
devotion to their employer's interests always meet
with their deserved reward, and well ! perhaps, he
was a widower : and perhaps the wife he had lost
had been the daughter of a well-to-do farmer, while
living she had watched over the friendless, innocent
country girl—had seen that she never went out
alone, and taken care that she was never out of safe
hands ; in fact, had been a true and honest sheep-
dog, and kept the wolves off from the stray lamb.
The widower is doing right, and just what his lost
wife would have wished him to do in marrying the
girl she so carefully brought up. She will look
after his house and property when he ventures out
on a holiday.

IRISH PEOPLE.

To the poet's eye the faces of his fellow creatures
all bear the stamp and impress of that first beautiful nature which the Great Being who created us
set upon his creatures ; on some, vice and crime and
evil habits have distorted the fair lineaments, but it
is only a temporary and chronic distortion—it will
fade away and leave them beautiful and calm in
death. All the anguish and the pain and sorrow is
smoothed away from the calm cold face when death
—not the terrible avenging angel—but the sweet
reliever, has ironed out the wrinkles. As Longfellow
sings—

> " Safe from temptation, safe from sins' pollution,
>   They live whom we call dead."

The jolly, laughing Irish flower girls who line the
railings of the Duke of Wellington's Statue may
seem to some a noisy, boisterous crew, throwing their
chaff about and exchanging rough jokes with the jolly
omnibus cads and cab drivers. In reality they are
full of their wild Irish fun, good and loving to each
other, perfectly happy and contented, knowing that

if any of them are taken ill they will be nursed and tended and carefully provided for. They generally ask fourpence or sixpence for a good flower for the button-hole; I always tender a penny, and accost them in their native Irish, "Ma cuishla machree. don't be too hard on a poor man." They always pass the word "Give the poor Sassenach jintleman a penny flower." So with the jolly omnibus drivers and cads; when a stoppage takes place, an outsider would think they were all angry, and that the rough language was the outburst of rage and ill humour; nothing of the sort, it is all done on purpose to rest their horses and let them catch their wind. The oaths mean nothing, as Uncle Toby said, "Our army swore terribly in Flanders." When a cabby is taken ill, a "benefit" is arranged at some special house of call of the fraternity, and every one contributes his quota in singing comic songs, or proposing some sentiment; a hat is then handed round and subscriptions pour in.

THE POET.

THE POET.

THE poet Longfellow has beautifully said —

> " O what a glory doth this world put on,
> To such as go forth with a quiet mind,
> And look on duties well performed,
> And days well spent."

This is indeed true; the heaven born Efflatus blows not save on those who lead a pure and good life. There must be no inner consciousness of guilt or sinful thought, no dimming of the light that shines upon the soul, no backsliding or hankering after the follies and frivolities, ambitions and vain desires of our fallen nature, no straying aside into the paths of pleasure, none of the shades that overhang those paths, no groping in the dismal darkness and rayless night that soon descends on those murky caves to which those paths lead. Art is a jealous mistress, she soon deserts her worshipper if he does not devote himself to her alone. The true artist finds pleasure in the simplest detail, and even the merest mechanical portion of his work, even the stretching the canvas on the frame, and the stippling and filling-in, are sweet and pleasant occupations. So

with the poet, to him the mastering of the different
languages in which poets of other nations sing is a
pleasure and no labor. His clear sense of hearing
soon detects the cousinly ring that can be traced
through all and every language. He will see at
once that the "leute" of the Teutons is the
"lioudi" of the Russians and Poles, that the braid
Scots' "fremmit folk" is only the "fremde folk" of
the Germans, that the "penge and siller" of the
Norwegians and Swedes is the "siller and penny"
of the Aberdonians, that the karohyi and kardyine
(king and queen) of the Hungarians is the Carolus
and Carolina of the Frankish Latins, and that the
German Karl is the same merging into Charles and
Siarl in Celtic. Thus the poet finds pleasure in
everything. What to others seem vulgar and
commonplace, to him is full of beauty and goodness.
When he walks into the city and strays amid murky,
mammon-gathering slums, where greedy men most
love to congregate, where thieves do break in and
steal, he thinks of "The Merchant of Venice," and
his argosies and carauls long due.

BLOOMING GIRLHOOD AND SAD SPINSTERHOOD.

BLOOMING GIRLHOOD AND SAD
SPINSTERHOOD.

One of the saddest sights to me is the enormous number of girls destined to old-maidship. It ought not to be so, and a kind Providence never meant it to be so, but our unnatural and artificial state of existence has brought this highly undesirable result about. While the prairies of the Mighty West, interminable, illimitable, exhaustless, are beckoning the down trodden millions of Europe across the Atlantic; while the uplands of South Africa, swarming with game, perfect in climate and temperature, offer every possible inducement to the young to start on the road of a self-reliant, hard working life, trusting in Providence for their future, our timid youths fear to take the first plunge, and stand shivering on the brink. How sad it is to see the countless. fine young fellows lounging away their time and ruining their health at the bars of restaurants and wine shops, or consorting with blacklegs, gamblers, touts, and ring-men of petty race courses, where leather plating is carried on by the rogues and money lenders, who own the weedy screws that can scarcely carry the feather weight that bestrides for half-a-mile, and yet these young fellows see some strange glamour-like charm in these unworthy and degrading pursuits. You cannot touch pitch without being defiled! and too soon the company they keep and the pursuits they follow tell their tale, confirm them in evil habits, demoralize and corrupt their whole nature, and instead of fulfilling their mission here on earth and obeying God's command, "Go forth and multiply!" they slowly descend into the downward road until they reach the drunkard's grave. Alas! how different had they been under a a stern course of discipline from seventeen to eighteen, under the colors, where they would have learnt habits of order, method, sobriety, and good conduct; another year in a merchant's counting house, or a lawyer's desk, in a barrister's chambers, or an engineer or manufacturing workroom, would have taught them the dignity of labour and the happiness that steady industry and useful occupation ever bring. Thus qualified for this work-a-day world, they might marry the first sweet girl that smiles upon them. Let them not wait for money, position, family, or any other selfish consideration, for "hope deferred maketh the heart sick," and long engagements frequently sap the health and lay the seeds of delicacy in fair and tender maiden. England ought to be like Holland, where it is a rare and

exceptional case to find a family of which at least one
of its members is not in far off Java, Sumatra, or
Celebes, or, as they are styled, the Dutch East Indies,
making or having made a comfortable independence.
But no! nothing will stir these idlers and street
loungers, or wake up their energy; and yet 'tis
pity, too. Most of the young men were originally
endowed with the choicest gifts of Providence:
health, strength, spirit, education, kind and loving
parents. 'Tis not getting into the right groove in
early life that does it. One year's idleness lays the
axe at the root of industrious habits, and these once
lost or unacquired, will not be recalled or obtained
easily.

"Where once such fairies dance, no grass will ever grow."

No less sad is it for the poor girls; the blooming
lass, that laughed upon Tom with her bonnie black
eye, waits on, month after month and year after
year, dragging their slow length along. Soon she
loses her health and spirits, her first charming
freshness of color and brightness of eye. Tom gets
from bad to worse, and is finally forbid the house.
How different, had Tom gone into the ranks for a
year when he left school, made a friend and confidant
of his officer, who would have befriended and made
him marry the girl at once, if she was honest and
good, and seen him and her safe on board a clipper
for Quebec, or Melbourne, or Sydney, or Adelaide,
or Brisbane. Ah me! what a different tale would

both then have had to tell—hard, unceasing work, galloping stock horses across the bush, overlanding a mob of cattle, clipping wool for dear life, or holding the plough stilts and guiding the bullock team between the stumps, and home to the rough shanty or shingle-roofed hut, where the bonnie wife and sweet bairns await him with looks and words of love. Turn we to a still sadder scene. What means those poor, painted, draggled creatures, that throng our streets? They have been betrayed, deceived and abandoned; their bursting heart has lost its faith in all that is good. Her lover has deserted her; "she gave him all she could," and now—

> "When lovely woman stoops to folly,
>   And finds, too late, men can betray,
> No charm can soothe her melancholy,
>   No art can wash her guilt away.
>
> The only art she can discover,
>   To hide her guilt from every eye,
> To give repentance to her lover,
>   And wring his bosom—is to die!

And yet these poor creatures are not altogether evil. I have seen them in the police courts—when "run in" for a general skirmish and scratching of faces of the sisterhood—when locked up for the night, kissing each other, and promising to bring a shawl and cloak and cup of tea in the morning. These poor things should never be rudely or roughly spoken to; their lot is indeed sad; short and wild and reckless in their career, the demon drink, and the sense of shame ever returning to the most hardened, soon bring them to the pauper's grave. Better indeed had it been for the man who has betrayed them, " that he had hanged a millstone round about his neck."

LINES ON A REFORMATORY.

LINES ON A REFORMATORY.

Flaunting by the flaring gaslight,
　　Shrieking wildly words of sin;
Eyes with scorn and phrenzy wild bright,
　　Lips all parched with fiery gin.

Wearied, worn, she sighs for slumber,
　　Sinks at last to fitful sleep,
Grieving o'er her care and lumber;
　　Unseen angels watches keep.

Wasted soon with sore disease,
　　Lost her once alluring smile;
Vain are now her arts to please,
　　Vain each often practised wile.

Stricken down with fever's stroke,
　　Soon her thoughts turn back to home,
Then within her conscience woke,
　　" Hence I must for aye to roam."

In her dreams her mother spoke,
"Daughter! rise, and don thy cloak ;
Homeward wend thy weary way,
Tarry not, nor longer stay ! "

Yonder cottage, thatched in sight,
Through the window beams a light ;
Softly o'er the gravel treads,
'Mid the trim kept garden beds.

Through the lattice eager peeps,
There her mother vigils keeps ;
Mother—yes, unseen the while—
Yes, 'tis she, the old sweet smile.

And there she sees the old arm chair,
Her sorrowing mother still sits there ;
She smiled upon her children there,
And breathed forth many a heartfelt prayer.

Upon the old deal table,
   A book before her lay ;
To read no more she's able,
   But there the book must stay.

That book whose sacred page
   Was once so careful conned ;
Her eyes now dim with age,
   But of the book she's fond.

A mark one page doth note,
   Let not the scoffer spurn,
A simple tale there wrote,
   " The Prodigal's Return."

Long the weary wanderer stood,
Veiled her face in down drawn hood,
Lifts the latch and ope's the door,
Fainting sinks upon the floor.

" O Mary! is it you, dear ?
   Safe, safe at home !
Come to my arms, my daughter,
   Thou wilt no longer roam."

" O, mother ! 'tis not meet
   For such as me to rise,
To foreign lands my feet
   Must turn, and foreign skies."

" Rise, daughter, rise, in slumber
   A sleep of death thou'st slept,
But all the while a number
   Of angels round thee kept

" A wakeful ward and watching,
   And while my daughter slept,
By them, with love unmatching,
   Daughter ! thy place was kept.

" I only know my daughter's safe,
   Returned to me at last,
Her sins and sorrows over,
   Her troubles all are past."

TICHBORNE.

TICHBORNE.

Among the "causes célèbres" which have puzzled the lawyers, nothing for many years has so exercised the disputatious powers of the public mind as the Tichborne Trial. It has been not a nine days' wonder, but a riddle to be read and an enigma to be solved ever since it was first broached in 1870. No one has ever yet known the real rights of the case, while the true key to it all lay right under our noses, so to speak. Many reputations have been shattered, and an absurd amount of animus and feeling thrown into it which was quite uncalled for. Dr. Kenealy has had somewhat hard measure dealt out to him, but he unquestionably labored under an honest conceit that his client was the real man. So did Mr. Whalley, also a thoroughly honest man ; so did Guildford Onslow. Had the good Doctor been as much among horses and horse dealers as the writer, he would have held the key and read between the lines, and all that seemed so puzzling would have been clear as the day. If he wants to be enlightened, let him read a report of the celebrated

horse case, tried at Shrewsbury, Lent Assizes, in
March, 1868, the case of Cox *v.* Greenwood, tried
before the Lord Chief Baron Kelly and Mr. Justice
Willes.   In that case, Cox, a horse dealer, sued an
iron master of Wolverhampton, named Greenwood,
for damages for false imprisonment.   It appeared
Mr. Greenwood had lost a five year old mare out of
his field.   The police arrested a man who was found
selling an animal so like the last animal in question,
that Greenwood and his grooms swore to it as being
the identical animal.   At the trial some seventy
witnesses all swore stoutly that it was the mare, some
seventy on the opposite side also swore equally
stoutly that it was not.   The trial lasted two days,
and every one, including judges, jury, and counsel,
were all persuaded that frightful perjury had been
committed; on the contrary, in reality, every one
spoke the truth.   The facts are very simple, and the
key to it was very simple.   It is an old trick among
Irish horse dealers, and is also practised among the
Affghan and Persian dealers.   A perfect brood mare,
like a perfect-bred short-horn cow, will throw to the
same horse, year after year, foals so exactly like to
and resembling each other, that none but a practised
eye can tell the difference.   The dealer and breeder
who had sold the five year old mare to Greenwood
had railed over her own sister, a year younger, and
the mare found by the police was a year younger;
the real animal, the five year old, was smuggled

back to Ireland; thus every body was right, and
yet every body was wrong. So in the Tichborne
case. The sham, big fellow, the "distressed
nobleman" at Dartmoor, was a bye-blow of old
Tichborne, and had got to know all the family
history. The good Doctor will see this when he
calmly runs this over and analyses all the facts of
the case. He will then, like the good fellow he is at
bottom, apologize to the Chief Justice, one of the
kindliest and most noble minded gentlemen that
ever adorned the bench, and that gentleman will
show the good Doctor that he had no option or
alternative save to rebuke him when he impugned
the integrity of the bench, and if the good Doctor
had been his own brother, no other course was open
to him. The Doctor should have thrown up his
brief after the two first days of the defence, and
when Luie came over, with his sackful of lies, then
the Doctor might have retired gracefully, and with
credit to himself. There is, however, a piece of
evidence which was never brought forward, but
which is quite conclusive to my mind as to the gross
imposture practised. A friend of mine happened to
stroll into the hotel where the impostor was sitting
smoking; my friend has a peculiar voice, which
subsides into a shrill treble, not to say a squeak,
when excited or laughing; now he has or had a big
brother who had formerly been in the Carabineers,
but he has a big, strong voice, not at all peculiar,

but after my friend left the room, the defendant asked the waiter " If that gentleman who had just gone out was not ——— ? " adding, " I remember him by his voice." Now it was quite evident he had learnt by the army list that ——— had been in the Carabineers, but he mistook the one brother for the other, and he thought it would be good evidence to say he remembered him by his voice. *Voila tout.* Thus we may say in the words of the poet—

> " Who the dickens Tich could be
> Half puzzled many a learned elf,
> Till lo ! they learned—O wondrous fact—
> That Tich was second self ! "

The judges are met—a terrible show,
The claimant and friends are all ranged in a row ;
The big wigs are baffled, and fierce grows the fight,
But justice shall triumph, and wrong sha'nt be
    right.

Sure purjury's rife, but murder will out,
Out of lies will come truth, though the swearing is
    stout ;
And th' imposter is hurried straight off to Dartmoor,
Whence 'tis hoped he will puzzle the world never
    more.

ON EARLY MARRIAGES.

ON EARLY MARRIAGES.

" Non cuivis contingit adire,
Vincula conjugii felicis."

To few indeed falls the happy lot of being happily
united in early youth to their first love. To realise
such a blessing, when the affections are fresh and
free, and the milk of love and kindness unsoured
by the gall of bitterness and disappointment, is a
spectacle too joyous and full of beauty to be often seen
on this earthly stage. Were it more common, as it
was no doubt meant to be, then indeed this world
would be a veritable Garden of Eden. Such
spectacles, however, are now and then to be seen;
very beautiful indeed are they to the spectators
whose hearts are big enough to enjoy the sight of
human happiness. I have myself had the pleasure
and privilege of knowing some such. Several of
my college friends, noted for their feats of strength
and reckless daring, after taking their degree, were
not "rusticated," but voluntarily went to rusticate,
there they met that blooming country girl that poets
love to sing of, and whom artists love to limn. One

" kissed the gamekeeper's daughter," another loved
" the miller's maid." In each case the voice of
nature cried aloud, and with a voice so shrill that
he could not choose but hear. But in each case the bold
lover showed himself a gentleman and an honest
man ; he took the wilding hedge rose to his bosom,
had it cared for, cultivated and tended, that is, he
educated and with culture and accomplishments
prepared his timid gentle wife for the position he
had raised her to. Verily, virtue hath its reward,
even in this life, though not always immediately or
directly. In each and every case lovely children,
running over with health and strength, blessed the
honest gentleman's home. With the "lowly lady"
hard work became a necessity, as the parents were
at first obliged to be kept in the dark, and they
naturally would only find the supplies for their son,
on the scanty scale of a bachelor's needs. Time is
the reconciler as well as the avenger. The old
people at length bewailed their son's virginity, and
went so far as to tell him that sooner than die without seeing him mated with someone, they would be
only too glad if he would marry some of the ripe-
lipped, black-eyed farmer's daughters. Then the
time had come—in one case an old college friend,
in another the publisher for whose magazine the
young benedict wrote, gently and judiciously broke
the news ; the beautiful, blooming children did the
rest ; and when the proud old parents and haughty

relatives saw the gentle, modest mother, and saw that on her nature had set her seal—*lady*, they also took her to their arms, saying, " Thou art one of us." Nevertheless, it is not always so. First impressions and love at sight are but soft stuff and sliding sand out of which to build the edifice of a life of happiness. That house must have its foundations laid on the primæval rock of goodness and purity, they will not deceive, and every maiden gifted with these will wear a face that, though plain and homely to the outer world in its expression, is beautiful to those who are also pure and good. It is best, perhaps, to keep away from the rustling white muslin, and the bright eyes and laughing looks, for they are apt to make wild work with the plodding brain, and lead him sore astray. We can but humbly pray with old Chaucer—

" Christ, keep these birdies bright from harm."

ON SCHEMING AND MEDDLING
WOMEN.

ON SCHEMING AND MEDDLING WOMEN.

It is an old saying and trite truism, that women are at the bottom of all mischief. This is, however, not true of kind, good, gentle women. Nowhere are the other sort more intensely mischievous than in regard to appointments in the army and church-militant. Nothing is more beautiful and adorning to a kind and gentle Christian minister than the crown of his household—a modest, matronly partner in all his cares and toils. She only leaves her nursery and household duties to tend the sick, visit the poor, make broth for the weak and hungry, and cut out flannel petticoats for the old women. Nothing on the other hand is more offensive, irritating, or ridiculous than a she-parson, a she-dean, or a she-archdeacon. Fortunately they are "raræ aves," but like pigs, when they try to fly, they make very odd birds. Anthony Trollope, in one of his inimitable novels, has depicted with great gusto and graphic power a clerical female of this genus. They are generally vulgar and self-asserting in style and manner, and if one took the trouble of tracing back their antecedents, they would be found to have

been originally a person (not a young person) who
had, after much angling after piscatorial prey in the
cathedral cities, succeeded in landing some honest
but weak minded old college don, who was induced,
much against his will, to forswear celibacy.   Alas
poor benedict !   His irrepressible partner is never at
rest until she has bothered the poor man into what
she calls "putting forward his claims."   No back
stairs are too steep for her, no stone too heavy to
turn.   Unfortunately ministers and dispensers of
patronage are courteous and good natured.   It is a
mistake.   The nearest boot to throw at her head
would be much more germane to the matter.   No one
save a badgered minister can realise the unblushing
effrontery and impudent persistance of this sort of
cut and come again old campaigner.   Like the
unjust judge, he at length gives in, because "she
importuneth me."   The same specimen used to be
found haunting the Horse Guards.   Sir Walter
Scott, in "Waverley," has hit off a sketch of the she-
dragoon.   The blunt, brave old soldiers, who used to
sit at the Horse Guards, dreaded her as much as
poor Captain Cuttle did the awful Mrs. McStinger,
or Bob Sawyer did his fearful landlady, Mrs. Raddles.
Almost all the bad appointments made have been
made under this pressure, sorely against the wills
and better judgment of the honest old generals, who
like to reward merit, and have always a soldier's eye
for the stuff that make good and brave soldiers.

Here again their courteous, chivalrous politeness to a woman is quite thrown away. When this sort of fox has once taken to haunt their poultry yard, they ought to loose some rough old mastiff, say a Scotch drum major or piper, with orders to him to begin to skerl a pibroch directly the vixen begins to throw her tongue. If he is not to the fore, let her mill-clapper wag on, and let the prudent old soldier observe a silver silence. As the cynical old trainer said, " Women is rum stock, they can't bear a walk over." I say " used to was," for the present commander-in-chief, God bless him, is the soldier's friend, and his selections are proofs of a diagnostic and penetrating eye. Sir Colin Campbell, Lord Napier of Magdala, and Sir Garnet Wolseley are the sort of men he picks out, and they do him credit. He knows that soldiers are like hounds, they will follow the best huntsmen, and if they find he does not know his business, they will soon drop their tails and lose their dash.

DREAM AND DEATH OF
THE LATE
SAMUEL WILBERFORCE, BISHOP
OF WINCHESTER.

DREAM AND DEATH OF
THE LATE
SAMUEL WILBERFORCE, BISHOP OF
WINCHESTER

(TRANSLATED FROM THE SEE OF OXON).

Rock-founded fortress, rest thou still,
Calm and serene upon thy hill,
In perfect trust await God's will,
Thy sons keep watch and ward!

And shall they pull down Church and State?
    In vain, in vain they'll try;
There's twice five hundred thousand men
    Will know the reason why!

Thou shalt enlarge thy borders,
    Extend thy vast domain,
And divers holy orders,
    Shall own thy holy reign.

Wide as the poles asunder,
   Yet one in faith and truth ;
O never ceasing wonder,
   They join in peace and ruth.

Wesleyans, baptists, quakers,
   Shall cast aside their rage,
And wild unreasoning shakers
   Their wrathful mood assuage.

John Knox is there, but gone
   The rigours of his brow,
Of all his sternness none
   Is left remaining now.

Wild zealots, fierce fanatics,
   Old covenanter's grey,
Clasp hands with mitred abbots,
   In mixed but bright array.

Behold, in sweet communion,
   The martyred dead are seen,
And Paris' murdered prelates,
   Waving their palm boughs green.

St. Peter bids the Peri
  Of Paradise unlock
The gates, and make no query
  What creed, what faith, what flock ?

She ope's her portals wide,
And none she thrusts aside,
Rolls free salvation's tide,
For all the Saviour died !

But softened are their features,
  Yet all aflame their eyes ;
These were once fellow creatures,
  They habit now the skies.

*　　*　　*　　*　　*　　*　　*

I see it, but not now,
  Behold it, but not nigh,
How plain and clear, I trow,
  To faith's keen piercing eye !

The dewey eve was freshening,
  The downs so dun and dry,
The dead man's placid face
  Gazed upwards on the sky !

The Church had lost her leader,
  She shed no tear of sorrow,
Solemn she said (God speed her),
  " How brightly breaks his morrow."

" No carv'd stone we will rear,
  We'll raise no sculptured urn ;
Let's place him on his bier,
  And homewards sadly turn."

Thus passed away our hero,
  In death's embraces cold ;
Our spirits were at zero,
  Our thoughts to none we told !

Let not the cynic sour,
  Or Puritan reprove,
His love of courtly bower,
  His humour's sportive grove.

To pure all things are pure,
  Religion's full of cheer ;
Relax thy front demure,
  And shed a kindred tear !

FINIS.

www.ingramcontent.com/pod-product-compliance
Lightning Source LLC
Chambersburg PA
CBHW030122030726
47498CB00007B/2500